For Frances

blue
moon
day

www.randomhousechildrens.co.uk

ANNE FINE

blue
moon
day

CORGI

BLUE MOON DAY

A CORGI BOOK 978 0 552 57188 3

First published in Great Britain by Corgi,
an imprint of of Random House Children's Publishers UK
A Penguin Random House Company

This edition published 2014

1 3 5 7 9 10 8 6 4 2

The Random House Group Limited supports the Forest Stewardship Council® (FSC®), the leading
international forest-certification organisation. Our books
carrying the FSC label are printed on FSC®-certified paper. FSC is the only
forest-certification scheme supported by the leading environmental organisations,
including Greenpeace. Our paper procurement policy can be found at
www.randomhouse.co.uk/environment.

Set in Bembo 13/15pt & Avenir Roman 12/14pt

Corgi Books are published by Random House Children's Publishers UK,
61-63 Uxbridge Road, London, W5 5SA

www.**randomhousechildrens**.co.uk
www.**totallyrandombooks**.co.uk
www.**randomhouse**.co.uk

Addresses for companies within The Random House Group Limited can be found at:
www.randomhouse.co.uk/offices.htm

THE RANDOM HOUSE GROUP Limited Reg. No. 954009

A CIP catalogue record for this book is available from the British Library.

Printed and bound in Great Britain by CPI Group (UK) Ltd, Croydon, CR0 4YY

I didn't want to go. Is that so odd? Sometimes you just don't feel like shlepping all the way to school to spend a whole day listening to the same old nagging from the same old people.

'Can you please open your workbooks.' 'You won't find the right page while you're staring up at the ceiling like that, will you, Felicity?' 'Take off that scarf, Gurdeep.' 'Are you *eating*, Robert? Put it in the bin.' Bleh, bleh. Bleh, bleh . . .

When I was really young I used to get to take a day off every now and again. I never pushed my luck. I had an excellent attendance record. I *liked* my primary school. But once in every blue moon, I don't know why, I didn't want to go. So I'd start moaning about having a pain in my stomach, or a headache or something. My mum would put on that wry look – the one that means, 'I'm not sure I believe you're feeling quite as bad as you make out, but I can't prove it and you're usually very good . . .'

So she'd let me stay home. I'd slop about, not

1

even dressed. Mum works in a corner of the living room, using the phone and computer to fix the daily schedules of minders who take care of all the old people on her patch. If I distracted her, she'd say, 'I wonder if you would get better faster if you went back to bed . . .'

I would stop irritating her at once.

I *loved* those days at home. Sometimes, of course, I'd find out next morning that I'd missed something really good at school. But not that often. And as Mrs Tyler next door says each time she sneaks off to climb Filbury Topping, everyone needs the occasional break in routine.

And we'll be getting our own soon. Dad's coming home. He's in the army so he's away for weeks on end, sometimes whole months. Everything's different after he comes home. I can't quite explain why, but though Mum and I seem to be able to run through our days easily enough together, when Dad walks through that door, it's as if he brings a scattering of grit into our family machine.

Don't get me wrong. I love my dad. And I admire him. All of his mates say he's a brilliant soldier. It's just that, before he comes home, I get a little tense. I start to chew my nails again. I worry that he'll pick on me for things I haven't done, or have done wrong. I know for sure Mum will stand up for me if she thinks that he's being unfair or unreasonable.

Still, I get tense.

So I don't care if I'm too old for what Mum used to call my 'blue moon days'. I felt like having one. To get it, I came down and stood behind her as she shook an avalanche of charred crumbs out of the toaster into the sink.

'My stomach's killing me.'

'What *sort* of killing you?'

'It really hurts.'

'You don't *look* very poorly.'

'You haven't even turned round! And for your information, I feel rubbish.'

She finally swivelled to face me. 'Oh, yes?'

'Yes!'

'Sam, this isn't a very convenient day for you to be off school.'

'Oh, sorr-ee! Sorry that I can't pick the very best time to feel so terrible.'

'*How* terrible?'

Since I'd begun the performance, I'd pretty well convinced myself I was in agony. I clutched my stomach. '*Really* terrible. Honestly. I feel as if whole chunks of me are falling out.'

Mum sighed and looked at the calendar. 'This

is a busy day for me. Are you *sure* you can't go?'

I suddenly felt guilty. There on the calendar were lots of little black squiggles, some even spilling backwards into yesterday or over into tomorrow. I realized it was the one day in the month when Mum drives round her area to check that all the minders she sends out are doing their jobs right. She'd made a heap of appointments for the day, and some of her old people get confused when things are switched around at the last minute.

'I'll be all right at home here by myself.'

It was quite obvious that wasn't going to wash. Hastily I added, 'Or I could come with you and stay in the car.' (After all, what did I care? Off school's off school. And even with those squiggles on the calendar, I didn't think that we'd be out all day.)

'I thought you said that you felt really sick.'

'No. What I said was that my stomach hurts.'

Now she was looking anxious. 'But you won't throw up?'

'What, in your nice clean car? I'll take a bucket with me, just in case.'

I was just being *sarcastic*, but she nodded, satisfied. 'Right, then. Go and get dressed while I call the school. Be ready to go in five minutes.'

Just as I reached the stairs, she called, 'And don't

bother bringing any waste-of-time computer games. Even if you're off school, you can be doing something sensible, like reading. And so I know that you're not cheating, you can leave all your screens behind and bring an old-fashioned *book*.'

'Come *on*!' I said. (I was outraged.) 'I am not faking it. I'm really ill.'

'Oh, yes,' she said. 'And I believe you. Now just hurry up!'

I knew she would be out of the car most of the time, so I slid my Stellar IV into my pocket anyhow, to keep me going till she crept up on me from behind and caught me at it with: 'What did I say? No stupid, waste-of-time games!'

After that I would really need something to read.

And there was nothing. Absolutely nothing. I looked along the shelves and couldn't see one single book I wanted to plough through again. There were a few I'd never read, but I was sure there'd be a reason. Either I'd started and then hated them, or something else had put me off.

I'd taken too long to get dressed. Mum was already at the bottom of the stairs, yelling away. 'Sam! Sam! We have to go!'

She's ruthless, is my mum. The moment Dad puts on his uniform and leaves the house for his next tour of duty, she turns into a Sergeant Major herself. 'Sam! Get down here at once! If we don't leave this minute, I shall be late for my first visit!'

I know how much she worries about keeping clients waiting. So I just reached out for the nearest book I'd never opened before and ran downstairs. I slammed the door behind me. She was already in the car, gunning the engine. I slid in at her side, clutching the book. She leaned across to read the title.

'Away From Home? Who gave you that one?'

'Granny.'

'Is it good?'

'I don't know yet.'

'What's it about?'

'I don't know that either, since I haven't read it.'

'Don't you get smart with me. What does it say on the back?'

I turned it over. Nothing. I opened it and flicked the pages. Then I saw the contents page and groaned. 'Oh, no! Short stories.'

'Don't be so negative. Some of them might be good.'

'Oh, yes,' I said. 'And all your old people might be in a really cheery and grateful mood.'

We shared a laugh at that. The lights at the corner turned to green, and we were away.

★　★　★

At the first house on her list, she outmanoeuvred me. (Dad says that, as a forward-looking strategist, he isn't a patch on Mum. He says, if she'd been in charge of his brigade, they never would have had to abandon their patch of Helmand Province.)

'OK,' she said. 'Show me what's in your pocket.'

'What, now?'

She nodded.

'Here?'

'For heaven's sake,' she said. 'Stop stalling, Sam.'

She probably had one of Great-grandpa's old service revolvers hidden up her sleeve. I wouldn't put it past her. I handed the Stellar IV over.

'Enjoy your book,' she said.

And she was off.

I stared out of the window for a while. I watched a couple of raindrops race down the windscreen. I studied the hedge beside me. I inspected my blackened fingernail from when I trapped it in the door.

Then I got bored, and started on the first story.

Exile

I suppose I didn't really think that it would happen. They'd talked of it so often. I'd stood behind the door and listened.

'The trouble is that having a tutor come in for Rick two or three times a week is really not enough. He should be in a real school.'

'I worry too. But you keep saying there'll soon be enough of us out here to make it worth while for the company to build a school.'

'Not soon enough.'

'But the idea of sending Rick away makes me so queasy. He's still so young.'

'He's not that young. I started at Tower House at *seven*.'

'Things were different then.'

'They weren't *that* different, Emily. Getting the right education, and knowing how to manage in the world is still important.'

On and on they went, chewing it over. I reckon that the threat of being sent away to school had hung over me so long that, by the time they actually did decide, I'd learned to blot it out. I know Dad talked of sports I would be able to play, games I would learn. And Mum went on about how quickly the weeks would pass, and how soon I would fly back home for my first holidays. I must have made all the right noises when I answered them, but I paid no attention.

I didn't even count the days.

So that last morning came as a horrible shock. I hadn't even seen Hasan send off the trunk. I asked about it and Mum said, 'Oh, darling! That was shipped off weeks ago!'

I made a horrid face. 'And now it's me you're shipping off.'

'Oh, darling!' she said again. Her voice was wobbly, but she put on that Got-To-Be-Nice bright tone she uses through all the tea and drinks parties she has to organize. 'It's not like that at all! Daddy and I will miss you terribly! Every single day! But you'll get used to it, I promise. And you'll have lots of the sort of fun you couldn't possibly have here.'

She waved her hand as if to say that there was nothing in the miles of desert sand and rippling heat beyond the factory compound that could compare with what they'd managed to arrange for me – as if being locked up inside one of those damp boarding schools I'd seen in films was going to be a *treat*.

It was a weird drive to the airport. They both kept up some cheery chat about how many things I would be able to do at this Walthorp Manor place. 'You'll never be bored,' my dad kept saying. 'No one is ever bored in school in boarding school!'

I didn't laugh. Firstly, I didn't think the pun was funny. And secondly, I wasn't really listening to anything they said. My mind was racing. All I could think was things like, 'I've still got time to jump out,' and, 'If those big traffic lights by the racetrack are on red, I could just open the car door and make a run for it.' I reckoned I could hide in all the prickly scrub along the road, then make my own way home. I was quite sure Hasan and his family would let me live with them.

Then maybe Mum and Dad would get the message.

There weren't many people on the sides of the road. A few shrouded women. One or two raggedy children. Now and again I'd see a huddle of old men squatting in dust, playing some dice game. I stared as we swept past. Everyone looked so calm. If I could speak the language properly, I would have rolled down the window and shouted, 'Don't simply carry on as if today's nothing special! Make the most of it! You don't know how *lucky* you are to be allowed to just stay here and get on with your life!'

The flight was all right, I suppose. The screen

at my first seat was dead, but the air steward asked a woman busy on her laptop if she'd mind changing places, and her screen was fine. Because the plane was late in taking off, the stopover in Abu Dhabi was only forty minutes. 'Please, darling! Ring us from the lounge,' my mother had begged me. 'We'll stay awake, waiting.'

But I thought, 'No. I have a good excuse: there wasn't time. And if you were so keen on hearing what I have to say, you should have let me stay *home*.' (We'd moved a lot, but all the places that we lived did feel like home to me. And I'd known plenty of others my age whose parents worked for the same company, and lived in out-of-the-way places. Not many had been sent away to school. Some, like me, had had lessons at home from local teachers. Others were taught from courses you could get over the internet.)

On the last flight I got so nervous that my stomach clenched. I must have slept, though, as the journey didn't seem that long. After we landed, a stewardess made me wait till all the other passengers had left the plane, then took me off with her. The walkways were all freezing cold. We reached the airport halls and walked straight past the queues. It all went very fast. And suddenly I was being pushed towards a woman younger than my mum, with frizzy red hair. She was still panting.

'Hello,' she gasped. 'I'm Ruth. I help out at the school sometimes. I've come to drive you there. I'm lucky I even made it here! The traffic was horrendous. Absolutely *awful*.'

I knew about the traffic from the holidays we used to take in England before Gran died. I didn't see how anyone could be surprised by it. My dad would sit behind the wheel of our hired car, cursing the crawling lines of vehicles. 'It beggars belief! Each time we come, I think it can't have got worse, and it always has!'

After Gran's house was sold, we used to go to New York for our winter breaks. (That's where my mother grew up.) And in the spring, we would go anywhere my parents fancied – usually some-where hot if Dad was working somewhere cold, or to one of their favourite ski resorts if we'd been, as we were then, somewhere that was bak-ing hot.

So I had not been back to Britain for three whole years. I was astonished by the sheer *green* of it, but couldn't say the traffic seemed any worse. I didn't care, in any case. I'd have been happy for the drive to last a hundred years.

'That's it,' said Ruth. She pointed. 'See the chimneypots above the trees? That's Walthorp.'

She was taller than I am. I couldn't see a thing and wasn't going to hotch up in my seat. So I just waited. We turned off the road and down a twist-ing drive shadowed by trees.

I don't think I will ever forget my first sight of the place against the sky. The car burst out into a circle of sunlit gravel that I took for sand until I heard the crunch of it beneath the wheels.

And there was my new school.

I hated being there right from the start. I hated everything about it. I look back now and realize that what I hated most was feeling lonely all the time, but never being alone. The only time I could be halfway to certain no one was watching me was when I was in bed at night. And even then you had to wait to be quite sure that you could cry without being heard because some of the others mucked about for ages. They would wait till Lisa the Junior Matron had scolded the last of them into lying quiet, but then as soon as she'd turned out the light and gone away, they'd start up 'dormie-hopping'. Sometimes you'd have to wait for hours to feel safe, and even then you'd have to use your sheet to mop away the tears because you couldn't ever cry aloud, or even sniff. They would be on you in a flash.

Some of them were nice. 'Don't worry. Honestly, you will get used to it.' But others spread it around. 'You know that newbie in our class? Well, he's a *weeper*.'

Weepers were teased, the same way anyone who could be worked into a rage was teased – simply to pass the time. Some loudmouth who had nothing better to do would choose a victim and start to needle him. As the noise level rose, others around them used to stop what they were doing to watch. Sometimes you never even knew how the whole business began. You'd just come round a corner to find someone like Simon Carter clenching his fists and screaming at his tormentor, 'Stop it! You stop it! Stop *saying* that!'

George Tully was the smallest in the class, but had a way of swaggering that made him seem bigger. 'I can say what I like. It's a free country, Simon.'

'Listen, I wasn't bothering you. Why don't you just push off and leave me alone?'

That irritating grin. 'Oooh, touchy, touchy! No need to get so ratty.'

'I am not getting ratty!'

'Yes, you are. Your face has gone all red! You look like a tomato about to explode.'

On and on. Horrible to watch because you knew if you barged in to help – 'You're just a bully, George Tully. Leave Simon alone!' – it would be you he picked on next time.

Finally Simon would burst with rage. He'd flail away at George, who'd just dance backwards while poor Simon's arms thrashed uselessly, making him look a fool. George would be grinning in triumph. 'Now, now, Simon! Temper, temper!' Tears of frustration would spurt from Simon's eyes. And that was it. Game over.

George would wander off to find some other person to torment, and one or two of those who had been standing round would try to comfort Simon.

'You should ignore him. He's a *pig*.'

'He's not worth worrying about.'

'He's just a bully.'

(At least they never added, like in books, 'And bullies are always cowards at heart'. That is such *rubbish*, and it doesn't help.)

But being a weeper was even worse than having a quick temper because some people at Walthorp would tease you about almost anything. They would pretend to be friendly, then dig out just enough about your life to make their insults stick. You take Luke Linton. As soon as he found out which country I'd flown in from, he made my life a misery with all his jokes about how I lived in a tent and had a snake in a woven basket for a pet.

He would explain things to me all the time. 'See this, Rick? This shiny silver thing with knobs? Well, that's a tap. You twist it. See? And out comes water! *Magic*, isn't it?'

'Out there, that wet stuff falling from the sky. That's *rain*.'

'We call these "chips". Can you say that, Rick? *Chips*.'

He would pretend to see sand falling out between my toes when I took off my socks. He claimed my dad must have a dozen wives. But then he pushed his luck too far one day by calling me a 'Towel-head'. (He meant the keffiyeh that Arabs wear.) Arif was furious, and he and his friend Ralph told Mr Anderson. But that was really just another warning not to get cross, because from that day on they got it worse than me.

So there was nothing you could do except pretend you hadn't heard, or thought that it was funny. If you just lost it and burst into tears, the mean ones going round would jeer, call you a 'Weeper', then move on to find their next amusement.

One boy who started school on the same day as I did left after four weeks. But others managed brilliantly. Take Charles. Whenever Luke started teasing him, Charles spread his hands and wailed, 'Oh, don't torment me! I'm already miserable because of the stone beds and ghastly food. Say one cruel word to me and I shall have to peg my hanky up to dry!'

And they'd push off! I couldn't understand it! But that was Charles's trick. I couldn't play it too. And he was only fooling anyway, because the beds were fine, and I thought that the food was brilliant. Nor was Charles even weepy. (I know because we slept in the same dormitory and I had never seen his downie quivering in the night when I crept off to the cold lavatory to have a quiet night cry.)

It didn't help me that I hated all the sports at Walthorp. Maybe because I'm what my granny used to call 'a lonely only', I never got the knack of wanting to do things in groups. I might have been all right if we'd done running or hurdling. I'm sure I could have trailed in last in a race or stumbled over a hurdle, and no one would even have noticed, let alone cared. But if I missed a catch at cricket or I fluffed a goal, the cat-calling would echo over the field. They jeered at me no more than at anyone else for being butter-fingered. But it annoyed me more. I think that even then I loathed what the teachers kept call-ing 'teamwork'.

By now you'll think, why was I even still at Walthorp Manor School? Why hadn't I just told my parents that I hated it and wanted to come home?

I can't explain. I think at first it might have been because I thought they'd make me stay in any case. 'Just long enough to see if you get used to it.' But then that other new boy left, and Tibor said quite casually next day when someone asked where he had gone, 'He wasn't up for it, so he went home.'

I suppose I didn't want to be 'not up for it' (whatever 'it' was).

But then, a few weeks into term, Charles begged to borrow my sharp purple felt pen. 'Just for a micro-minute.'

He wasn't kidding. It was only a moment before he'd handed it back. I looked over his shoulder to see what he'd been colouring. It looked as if it was one tiny dot on an enormous grid.

'What's that?'

'It's just my Chet,' he said.

'Chet? What's a Chet?'

He looked surprised I didn't know the word. 'Chart of the Hours to the End of Term,' he said. 'Usually I just do squares. But this year I've mapped the whole thing out in hexagons, and I am filling them in only in purple, pinks and blues.'

I looked more closely. There must have been about a hundred thousand tiny little pencilled six-sided shapes, all fitting neatly together like a patterned quilt for someone the size of your thumb.

'Did you rule all those out yourself?' I asked him. (I was amazed.) 'How long did *that* take?'

'Pretty well the whole of the last week of the hols. My mother got quite ratty. "What is the point of being home," she kept on saying, "if all you're going to do is sit there making a chart of all the hours of next term?"'

I pointed to the burst of colour down the left-hand side. 'Are those the hours we've already done?'

He tapped my head as if I were a woodentop. 'Doh! What else?' He peered at me more closely.

'Really, Rick, have you never seen a Chet before?'

I shook my head. 'I've never been away from home before.'

'Lots of us have them,' he explained. 'Look in the cubby holes. What's good about them is that, if you have a few good days, you don't go near them. Then, when you're miserable and time is dragging, you have a lot to tick off.'

'Still, every single hour! It must be *thousands*.'

'It is exactly twenty-four thousand and twenty-five hours,' Charles explained. 'Unless you leave half-term and the weekends out.'

I took another look at Charles's chart. 'So does it really help?'

He nodded his head in such an enthusiastic way that I almost believed him when he said, 'They do. They really do.' He pulled a fresh sheet from his pad. 'Why don't I make one for you? I won't have time to do it all in fancy hexagons like mine, so it'll have to be plain squares.'

'What, counting hours from today?'

'No. From the start of term. That way you'll have a block to colour in at once, to set you off.'

That sounded good. 'You're sure? Because I've got a calculator. I could do it myself.'

'No, no. I quite like making them. What time of day did you arrive?'

I thought back. The beginning of term seemed light years in the past. 'I do remember that the first meal I had here was tea.'

'We'll call it four o'clock, then.'

Off he went, cheerfully singing some old nursery song about a rabbit bopping people on the head. And I went off to change for games.

The Chet arrived a couple of days later. I found it in my bedside cubby, along with a brand-new pack of coloured pens that Charles must have bought for me from the school shop. I didn't want to make a mess of filling in the first four weeks, so I put what he'd given me back in the cubby, thinking I would find time to colour in the squares next day.

In fact, it was about a week before I got to it. (I don't know where the time went. I know I had to queue twice at the shop to buy the chocolate that I gave to Charles for making me the Chet. And I had just been chosen as the Duke of York in the school play. Some of the time we were all making puppets. And Charles had roped me into helping him make his stained-glass windchime in the craft room at any time I wasn't busy with my first lessons at chess club.)

But that day when I started on the chart had been a difficult one. George Tully had been irritating everyone all morning, especially me. He'd found a rubber snake and he'd been walking between the desks over and over, shoving it in my face and whispering, 'Have you lost your only desert friend?'

Next time I saw him coming, I stuck out my

21

leg, planning to trip him. Then Tibor whispered, 'Just ignore him, Rick. Wait till you see his dad.'

I drew my foot back, curious, and rather pleased that Tibor had been whispering to me as if I were a good friend. 'What's special about George's dad?'

Tibor rolled his eyes. 'Mr Tully's a really mean guy. And he is horrible to George.'

That cheered me up a bit. 'What sort of horrible?'

Tibor shrugged. 'You know. George can't get anything right. Nothing he does is ever good enough. His marks are far too low. He's not in the top teams.'

'I'll probably get that, too, when I go home.'

'Maybe.' Then Tibor added something that made me feel a little sick. 'Last term, when George's dad drove here to pick him up, he got out of the car and the first thing he said to George was, "You haven't grown much in twelve weeks!" '

I thought about that quite a lot during the afternoon. I know my dad would never, ever say a thing like that – especially not if I was small like George. (And, if he did, my mum would probably deck him with a frying pan. She hates mean people.)

As soon as I had finished painting freckles on my puppet's face, I went upstairs. We're not supposed to hang about the dormitories till after the last day bell's rung. But I just really wanted to be alone.

I filled in squares while I was thinking about home.

After a while I heard footsteps. Lisa. She stood in the doorway for a moment watching me, and then she said, 'Are you all right, Rick?'

I didn't trust myself to speak.

'Having a little quiet time all to yourself?'

I nodded.

'Is that your Chet? Nice colours! But you've got a way to go.'

'To the end?'

'No, to as far as we've got.' She put her finger down about a thousand hours away from where I was carefully filling in a yellow square under a green one. 'We must be about here by now.'

Her finger was pretty well halfway across the chart.

'Half term next week. Will you be going home?'

I shook my head. 'It's such a long way – and a lot of money. My mother wasn't sure if it was worth it just for a few days. She said that I could fly back if I really wanted. But I said that I didn't mind.'

'Goody!' she said. 'I love it when there's company over half term. There will be eight of you still here. What's nice is that we all eat

23

together, and you help me and Mr Fox paint the back cloth for the play.'

She moved towards the door.

'Oh, and we go to the cinema. And to that pool in town – that big one with the flumes. And we have films each night, with sausage rolls.' She pointed to my Chet. 'And you'll have plenty of time to get up-to-date with that.'

She said one last quick thing before she left. 'Don't stay up here too long.'

I thought that was a really nice way of saying, 'You shouldn't be up here at all.' I didn't want to get her into trouble, so I put all the caps back on my pens and shoved the Chet back in my cubby hole. There would, I knew, be plenty of time to get it done later.

And I had promised Charles a bit of help assembling his finished windchime.

He would be waiting downstairs.

I'd finished that first story when Mum came back. In fact, I'd started on the next, but couldn't concentrate. My mind kept drifting back to Rick. (I think that I was wondering how I'd have managed so far away from home.)

But suddenly there she was, wrenching the car door open and hurling herself into the driver's seat. 'God grant me patience!'

'Old Mrs Gray not happy with the service?'

'She's spitting tintacks!' Mum put on a quavery voice and wobbled her head from side to side. '"Those minders of yours! They don't know how to make a bed properly. Or vacuum a rug. They don't know how to make porridge. They never think to change the water in a flower vase."' She snorted. 'According to Mrs Gray, all they know how to do is prick and ping.'

'Prick and ping?'

'Stab a fork into a packaged meal and bung it in the microwave.'

'That's good,' I told her. 'Prick and ping. I shall remember that.'

That calmed her down. She grinned. 'So what about you?'

'Fine,' I said. 'Wagons roll?'

Mum took a look at the dashboard clock.

'Blimey!' she said. 'Was she complaining all that time? My golly! Wagons roll.'

The next stop was a bungalow beside a park. 'This one's dead easy,' Mum said. 'Adele Harris is a sweetie. Grateful for everything. I'll be back out in no time at all.'

'I expect you'll find me still here. Since I have absolutely no idea where we are, I probably won't run away.'

If you want my opinion, every bungalow in the world looks much the same as the next. I stared at Number 45 for no more than a minute before I got so bored that I went back to the second story in my book, *The Reading Challenge*.

The Reading Challenge

I won The Reading Challenge every year when I was in my day school. That is because I live at the back of nowhere – so deep in the country that if we have visitors, even with Satnav they get lost about ten times before they get to us, and by the time they do arrive they're often crotchety.

We can't move somewhere else. Dad's family have owned this house for over two hundred years, so there's no budging him. It's why Dad's first wife left. She said our valley was a 'one-eyed hole'. And even my Mum (she's called Marie-Hélène) can't stand the place in winter.

'Marooned again! I will go mad!' she says each time the winding roads get blocked with snow. We're always last to get the snow plough chugging past the gates, and even then the drive is still knee deep. Dad's far too old to clear it now. (Mum's his third wife.) And Mum won't do it. She prefers to complain.

So it was no surprise I always got through far more books than anyone else, and won the prize each year. With no one else my age around, what could I do but read? Mum bought a lot of books online to try to stop me grumbling. And in the town where she goes every two weeks to do the most enormous shop, there's a good library.

But now I'm at Glebe House, things are quite different. I still read almost all the holidays. In fact, I start off even before I've left the school. That is because it's Mum who comes to fetch me at the end of term, and she's the last to arrive. (Dad says that is because she's French, and the French think that being on time is rude.)

Whatever it is, her car is always – *always* – the last one to come up the school drive. I snap my book shut and jump off the wall in front of the boarding house. I run to Mrs Harper to get my name crossed off her Gone-Home-Safely list. Then Mum and I shove all my stuff into the car and off we go.

'How's Looper?' is my first question. (Looper's my dog.)

Mum pouts. 'Genevieve! It would be nicer to ask after Daddy first!'

But I don't worry about Dad. He knows exactly where I am, and when I'll be back. Looper is different. I vanish at the start of term and stay away till the first weekend out. He doesn't know I haven't abandoned him, and I've read all about what happened to dogs locked up in quarantine for months on end to check that they weren't coming down with rabies. Loads of them pined and pined, and then gave up and died of broken hearts.

That's why I worry about Looper. I ask again, and this time Mum admits he's fine in those clipped tones that mean, 'What else would you expect?' So then I know for sure that all those emails she's been sending me complaining that Looper chewed Dad's wellies into shreds, or barked at a hedgehog till he lost his voice, were really true, and not just lies to keep me happy till she gets me home and can tell me the awful news about his pining to death.

I sit back after that, perfectly happy. I know it takes two hours to drive home, and just so long as Looper can last through that he will be in my arms, tumbling and licking. Then I can beef up his spirits, tickling his tummy all the time I'm reading through the holidays so, when I leave again, he's tough enough to last till my first weekend home, or till half term.

So now I am relaxed enough to ask, 'Well, how is Daddy?'

'Daddy is fine. He's longing to see you, of course.'

It comes out, oh, so casually, that little 'of

course'. But I'm not sure I quite believe it. When I'm in school, I hardly think of Mum and Dad at all – well, sometimes at night when someone in my dorm is using my hair to practise their fancy plaiting. (Mum used to brush it for me, it's so long.) Or if I've quarrelled with someone and wish I could be miles away. And every time I email them, of course.

The rest of the time, I try not to think of home – mostly because of Looper. And I am certain that my parents are like that as well, except the other way round.

I know because, when I get home, I read their diaries.

Yes, yes. I know. That's *terrible*. But I read *everything*. And so would you if you lived here and you were me. You'd want to know whether they missed you, wouldn't you? And if there was no chance of being caught, I bet you'd do it too.

And it's a laugh. My dad is really, really old – more granddad age. He has the firm black italic handwriting that he was taught at school and keeps his diary entries very brief. A week might run like this:

Monday 8th: Coal delivered sopping wet – again!
Tuesday 9th: Dragged around bloody Waitrose by Madame. And what is 'pesto' anyway? It looks like chewed-up spinach.
Wednesday 10th: Chucked it down all day. No

chance of stepping out of the side door, let alone digging up spuds.

Then I'll root in Mum's desk while she's downstairs arranging flowers, and read her diary. She bungs in quite a lot of French, but I'm good at that now. My problem is she has that loopy French writing that's hard to decipher. I look up all the words that I don't know. And once I've sorted it out, I'll find my mum and dad live in two different worlds.

I'll look up Monday 8th, and she'll have written: *Still no coal!*

On Tuesday 9th, she might not even mention the trip to Waitrose. She'll write, *So worried about Maman. She has been quarrelling with Angelique again.* (Angelique is Mum's sister.) There will be half a page about how those two got in another spat. (That's usually the best bit. Once they fell out for two whole years over a borrowed milk jug.)

And then, on Wednesday 10th, when Dad was saying that it chucked it down and he could not set foot outside the door, Mum will have written: *A glorious day! Truly a gift from the gods! I went for a long, long walk on Hunter's Edge, and barely a spot of rain.*

They live in different worlds, truly they do.

When I come home, the first thing that I like to do is read their entries for the day I left.

Take last September. This was Dad's entry:

31

Marie-Hélène drove Genevieve back to Glebe House. I fear my tomatoes may have blossom-end rot.

Nice, eh? Most loving.

Then I'll read Mum's. *The end of the holidays. The traffic was fearsome.* (She has written 'affreux'.) *I must remember to drop G off much earlier in future.*

See? Why should I worry about them? They're obviously not worrying about me. (Or, if they are, it runs, as Mrs Alabaster says in English class, 'too deep for words'.)

So I just try to tell myself they know I'm happy at Glebe House and, if I wasn't, I would tell them so. And I am happy, just so long as I can keep myself from fretting about Looper. It was my decision, after all. As far back as I can remember I was begging them to let me go away to school. I had a passion for boarding-school books. I read all the Harry Potters and the Enid Blytons. Then Dad dug up a heap more about two boys in prep school who were called Jennings and Darbishire. (They were the best.) And then the lady in the library put me on to other books by Angela Brazil.

And I just nagged and nagged.

Dad kept insisting, 'You would *hate* it, Ginny! Honestly! I hated it from the first day to the last. It's an *unspeakable* fate.' Then he went on about cold showers and icy floors, and lavatories without locks. He even claimed that Matron poked her head inside each lavatory stall to check their poos before she'd let them flush.

I didn't believe him. Well, would you? I simply thought that he was trying to put me off – until his elder brother Ralph came to stay for a few days.

'Tell her!' said Dad. 'This foolish child here claims she wants to go to boarding school. Tell her what Matron did to us every morning.'

You could see Uncle Ralph trawling back through decades of memories. 'You mean, forcing us to swallow cod liver oil?'

'No, not that. What she did every morning in the lavs.'

'Oh, yes! She tore off two small squares of that hard, shiny paper for each boy. What was it she used to say? "Here you are. One square to wipe and one to polish."'

My mother laid down her fork. 'William! Ralph! This is neither the time nor the place for this conversation!'

'Sorry!' said Dad. Chortling, he turned to me. 'Still, you get the point, Genevieve?'

Uncle Ralph, meantime, had finished his lengthy brain search. 'Of course!' he said. 'Now I recall! After you'd finished, but before you were allowed to flush, she used to—'

'Enough!' Mum interrupted. '*Ça suffit!*'

Uncle Ralph echoed Dad's apology. 'Whoops!

Sorry, Marie-Hélène. Won't utter on the topic again.'

I said, 'But all that was a hundred years ago. Things are quite different now. There's no more icy-cold lino on the floors. It's all warm carpets and curtains. And no one sleeps in great long dormitories, like in your day. They sleep in much smaller groups. And lots of schools even have little private cubicles for everyone. And—'

For all he'd promised not to, Uncle Ralph uttered again. 'Ginny, don't even think of it! The sheer, mind-cracking tedium of it all! Boarding school means just that, you know. Bored in School! The absolute horror.' He leaned across the table as if to share a secret. 'That's why the captured British officers survived so well during the war. After the grim routine of boarding school, life in a prison camp was pretty well a cake-walk.'

'What is a cake-walk?' I asked.

Mum told me I had better google it, but Dad explained it was a kind of dance. So I chipped in again. 'But that's another reason why I want to go! You get to do all sorts of different things after school if you're a boarder. Games. Dancing and art. Choirs. Sewing clubs. Tennis. Putting on plays. All that I get to do stuck here is *read*.'

'But you *like* reading,' said my Dad.

'I know I do,' I said. 'But not every single free hour. Not all the time!'

Mum waved her hands about. 'No, no, Genevieve! I can't abide the thought! It's horrible! Only the English would bother to have a child and then send him or her away for other people to bring up! The very idea!'

But I kept at them, day after day, month after month. And in the end, Dad cracked. 'Look, Marie-Hélène, if Genevieve really, really wants to go, why don't we let her? She'll soon see it's horrible and want to come home again. What's to be lost?'

I knew then I had won.

It took another week or two to bring Mum round. Then Dad was firm with me. 'At every school I know, you have to give a full term's notice if you want to leave, or you still pay the fees. I'm not wasting that sort of money. So if we sign you up, and you turn out to hate it, you'll have to stick it out till at least Easter.'

After I promised that, it was a deal. And it turned out, of course, that several of Dad's friends had grandchildren in boarding schools. Phone calls and letters poured in. (Dad won't do emails or texts, except with me, and only then if Mum sets him up first.) So it was only a few weeks before the two of them drove me up to Glebe House to meet the head and look around.

Fabulous! Just what I wanted! Towers and courtyards and funny little rooms and corners. And dozens of girls my age pretending not to stare, but smiling at me if I caught their eyes. As we were closing one of the doors behind us, I heard a girl say, 'Did you see her *amazing* hair? She looks like Rapunzel!' And someone else gave me the thumbs-up sign as we went by. I had been feeling rather nervous until then. But that thumbs-up sign clinched it. So when we climbed back in the car and Dad said, 'Well, Genevieve? What is the verdict now you've seen the place?', I just leaned forward and said, 'Yes, please!' and kissed his shiny bald head.

'Careful,' he warned me, 'or you'll get a mouth-ful of hair.'

'Ho, ho.'

He turned to Mum, who always drives. 'And what does Madame think?'

Mum shook her head a little irritably. 'Well, if it stops her going on and on and on . . .'

'That's settled then. I will start growing cabbages at once.' He called back over his shoul-der. 'You realize, Genevieve, that cabbages are all we will be able to afford to eat, once we are paying those fees.'

I don't think I saw anything out of the window on the drive home. I just sat in a haze of joy.

I'm sure I was the happiest person in the school. From the first day they nicknamed me Rapunzel because I had the longest hair in school. After about a week they even shortened that, to call

36

me Punzy. I'm in the choir and I take extra classes in tap and salsa. Once a week Safira and I walk to the village hall to make tea for old people in the Memory Club, and every Tuesday afternoon our class goes skating at the local rink.

So I am always busy. Always. I've been here three years and I'm *never* bored.

Then last year Mrs Alabaster said the school was doing something new. The Reading Challenge. 'Once you've signed up, you read as many books as you can in three weeks.' She said we could get family and friends to sponsor us for every book we read to raise some money for our favourite charity. Or we could simply read.

'And there's a prize for the girl who reads the most books,' Mrs Alabaster finished up.

Emilia nudged me. 'Hear that, Punzy? A prize!'

'I know,' I said, and couldn't help adding, 'I won the Reading Challenge four years in a row in my old school.'

Netty was listening and I saw her give Emilia a little smile. Then, 'Really?' she said to me, as if she didn't believe what I'd said.

I blushed. 'Yes, really.'

I was about to explain that, when I was living all the time at home, there wasn't anything to do but read. But Netty got in first. 'You don't do that much reading here.'

'Well, that's because there isn't time. I'm always *busy*.'

And that is true. Even before you've woken properly, someone is chatting to you. There's always someone laughing and joking at break-fast. Then we have classes, and during breaks we mess about in groups. Even between the end of lessons and supper, I am forever rushing off to change for clubs, or sports, or dance class.

The teachers use up every other minute of the day. They can't walk past on the stairs without pouncing. 'Genevieve! Be an angel and take this note to Mrs Harris for me. I'm pretty sure she's in the hall.'

'That's not a class you're rushing to, is it, Genevieve? No? Good! Then can you run and tell the janitor that the front gates have stuck again, and Mr Crispin's waiting in his car.'

'Who isn't going to Drama? Genevieve! Save my poor feet and take this folder to the office, will you? And while you're there, please tell Miss Harper that I need another squared pad. Don't just give the message and rush off. Wait till she finds one and bring it back to me. I'll be in the staff room.'

See? How much reading would fit in with that?

Your friends keep you too busy for books all afternoon. 'Punzy, we need one more on Tiana's team. Don't be a spoilsport! Come on!'

'You understood that maths we did today? Truly? Can you explain it?'

'I want to tell you something really funny. Over here. Quick!'

And even in the dorm, I still can't get to read. They haven't named me after Rapunzel for nothing. They keep borrowing my hair.

'Please, Punzy. Katya wants to show how her half-sister plaits her hair for parties back in Moscow. She needs hair as long as yours or she can't do the topknot.'

'Keep your head still, Punz! Don't keep tugging forward.'

'Sorry, I'm going to have to start again. I got the parting wrong.'

No one could read through that. The print jumps up and down. You keep on losing your place. You find you've read the very same sentence ten times in a row, and you give up. So it was not surprising I didn't win the Glebe House Reading Challenge that first year. Caroline took the prize, and Jessica came second. But Caroline had a head start because she spent each weekend back at home after she broke her leg. And Jessica is really shy, and hides in the library.

But Netty noticed that I wasn't even in the top five. She kept on mentioning it, which was annoying enough. But when I went up on stage to get my plain old boring Reading Challenge certificate, I saw her smirking at me while she whispered something to Emilia.

Both of them grinned, but Netty did it in a

really spiteful way, that made me want to show her. That was why I made my solemn vow: next year, I'd win the prize just as I had each year in my old school. I'd do whatever it took – whatever! – just to show Netty.

I didn't think about it much till the spring term, and then I tried to organize things so I'd have a chance. First I asked Mrs Alabaster if we could shift the Challenge to the holidays. But she said every school held it over the same three weeks in term time to be fair to everyone who didn't have a library near them at home.

So then I asked if I could drop my clubs and extra dance classes during the Reading Challenge. Mrs Alabaster said no. My parents had already paid for them, so I must go.

Then she got curious and asked why I was fretting about something that wasn't happening till next term. I didn't see how I could answer without making Netty sound as spiteful as I thought she'd been, so I had to act dumb. Then Mrs Alabaster patted my shoulder and reminded me, 'The Challenge is supposed to be fun. It doesn't matter.'

But it did to me.

So when Mum drove me home and I had checked that Looper was alive and Dad was fine, I started on my cunning plan. Cradling Looper in my arms, I told Mum, 'This dog's getting fat.'

'Really? I hadn't noticed.'

I tried to concertina Looper up a bit, so he looked bulkier.

'Maybe a little plumper,' she admitted.

Then I went after Dad. 'These holidays I want to spend more time outside. Mum says that Looper's getting fat, so I am going to take him for long walks.'

'Anywhere in particular?'

I shrugged. 'Here and there. Walking about in the valley.'

'Looper will like that,' Dad said. 'I've always thought the poor creature doesn't get enough outings.'

'He will this holiday,' I warned.

And Looper did. On the first day, I walked him as far as the third cattle grid. That is a quarter of the way to the main road. The second day I walked him further. And the day after that, we went as far as the pig farm.

'You're out a lot,' Dad said at supper time. 'I've hardly seen you all day.'

'Walking,' I said.

Next day I walked Looper all the way to the main road. We reached the bus stop with the timetable. I copied some of the bus times down while Looper had a rest. Then we came home.

That night I read their diaries. Mum's said, *My little Genevieve is growing up. She mopes round the countryside all day like lovelorn Werther.*

I didn't know who Werther was and so I

googled him. He was some miserable bloke in a book who ended up topping himself.

Thanks, Mum.

Dad's diary said, *That mangy cat from the farm has scuffed up all my anemones. We don't see much of G, except at meals.*

I didn't reckon either of them seemed too worried about my change of habits. So I moved on to the next stage of my plan – asking for extra money.

'Extra?' my dad yelped. 'Ginny, have you the faintest idea how much that school costs? We're now poorer than church mice!'

But I was determined. 'You could give me my allowance in advance.'

He fished inside his wallet. 'I shall keep track,' he warned.

He raised his eyebrows when I told him how much I wanted. 'How could you possibly need that sort of money? There isn't a shop for miles.'

'Secret,' I told him. 'You'll soon find out.'

Next day, I packed a picnic lunch inside an old woven shopping bag. 'I shall be gone some time,' I told them.

'Bye, Captain Oates,' said Dad.

Before I left, I googled Captain Oates. That's what he said when he walked out into the snowy Antarctic wastes to die.

Nice one, Dad. Thanks.

Looper and I set off. We reached the bus stop

just in time. I stuffed him in the shopping bag and climbed on the bus. We sat right at the back and I let Looper raise his head so he could stare out of the window.

I stared out too.

It took us forty minutes to reach the town. We passed the Waitrose on the right, and I got off at the next stop.

And there it was. The hair salon. 'The Cut Above'.

I tethered Looper to a lamp post and pushed the door open. The place seemed busy, but the girl at the desk said someone would soon be free. 'What do you want doing?'

'I want it off,' I said.

She looked appalled. 'What, all that lovely hair?'

'Yes. All this lovely hair.'

'Oh, dear!' she said. 'It must have taken *years* to grow that long.'

'It did,' I said. 'And now I want it short.'

She was still worried. '*How* short?'

'Short enough not to be plaited.'

She tipped her head to one side, cheering up a bit. 'Sort of a bob?'

I wasn't quite sure what she meant. At school we say things like, 'As short as Sandra's hair', or 'Curly, like Alicia's'. But I didn't want her to think I was some sort of country bumpkin (even though I am) so I said, 'Yes, please.'

She called another stylist over. 'Glynnis, this young lady wants a bob.'

Glynnis's eyes gleamed. 'Fantastic! Has she come as a model?'

The first girl turned to me. 'Have you?'

I didn't know a thing about hairdressing salons. Up till then, Mum had done the trimming for me. So I said, 'I suppose so.'

'Oooh!' she said. 'All that long, lovely hair! This'll be good.'

You won't believe me but they took a set of photographs before they started. I didn't even know that was unusual, so I just smiled at the camera, then sat there quietly while they took more shots from the side.

Next I was led away to have my hair washed, and after that I just sat watching Glynnis clip away. Snip, snip. Snip, snip. She wouldn't let me turn my head, so every few minutes I would ask her, 'Is my dog all right?' and she would glance across and say, 'Nobody's stolen him yet.'

Sometimes she hummed while she worked. Sometimes she frowned. The hair fell around me, first in slinky heaps, then in short floaty bits as she trimmed round my neck and cheeks.

She used the hairdrier and a round brush to puff up what was left. 'Watch carefully,' she said. 'You'll have to do this for yourself when you get home.'

'There!' she said proudly at the end.

'It is too short to plait?' I checked with her when she held up a mirror so that I could inspect the back. 'You're *sure*?'

You could tell that she thought it was the oddest question. 'Yes,' she said. 'No one could possibly plait that.'

'Good!'

I started to slide off the chair but Glynnis pushed me back so she could take a few more photographs for what she called her Before and After portfolio.

At the front desk, I pulled out the money Dad had given me. That's when I saw the sign: *Want a Free Hair Cut? Come as a Model for one of our Trainee Stylists.*

Hastily I covered my tracks. 'Can I buy one of those round brushes Glynnis used on me?'

The girl pointed across the street. 'They sell them there. In Tupper's.'

'Right,' I said. 'Well, thanks! I'm really pleased.'

I crossed the road to Tupper's and went mad. I bought a rounded brush, a brand new hairdrier of my own, and cocktail sausages. (They were on special. It was the last day that they could be sold.) Looper and I ate all the sausages on the ride back. And then I made him walk all the way home from the bus stop.

My mother nearly fainted. '*Ma foi!* What have you *done*?'

'I think it's very cute,' my dad said. 'Stylish. You look a good deal older. Did it cost the earth?'

I won the Reading Challenge the next term. (So snubs to Netty.) I'll win it next year, too. I'm still called Punzy, even though no prince would stand a chance of climbing up Rapunzel's tower if her hair was as short as mine. I still get worried about Looper every now and again. But otherwise, my life could not be better.

I still read both their diaries whenever I come home. Last time, they went like this:

Mum, on June 28th: *A Cut Above this morning, and my hair looks wonderful. I will admit my clever Genevieve found a real gem in Glynnis.*

Dad, on the very same day:

Another ghastly morning traipsing around in that benighted town. My God, was I glad to get home!

Whichever diary I go by, we clearly won't be moving soon. But I don't care. I'm never, ever bored in school, and that makes up for living here.

Mum had said she'd be back in no time, but I had finished the second story well before she arrived.

Without a word she threw herself in the car and drove round the corner, pulling into the side again almost at once.

'That's handy,' I said. 'Our next stop?'

'No! I'm just so angry after that last visit I have to take a moment before I'm fit to drive.'

'You told me Adele Harris is a sweetie.'

'She is. But her great loaf of a son was there, to stick his nose in.' Mum almost growled. 'I don't know how he has the *nerve*. He only bothers to visit once a year, on his way north for his fishing trip. And all he does is crab. "Why are her clothes spread all around her bedroom? Why can't the minders unpack the food into the kitchen cabinets instead of leaving it about? And what has happened to those very expensive rugs that used to be in the front room?"'

We both fell silent. I know what I was thinking.

I was thinking to myself, That sounds like Dad the day that he comes home. Before he's settled in. Picking on everything and everyone. Not even bothering to ask the reasons for things, as if the two of us were squaddies who had been ignoring orders, not people who'd been managing fine all the time he wasn't here.

I took the tiniest sideways glance to see if I could guess if Mum was thinking much the same.

I couldn't tell. But since she stands up for herself in front of Dad, who looks quite scary when he's in a mood, I didn't think she'd have let Adele Harris's 'great loaf of a son' get away with much of anything.

And clearly she hadn't. 'I put him straight at once! I told him, "Your mother's clothes are spread around because, since your last visit over a *year* ago, her arthritis has got so bad she can no longer reach up to her closet hangers. The minders leave stuff on the kitchen counters because she can no longer bend to use the lower cabinets and she's so tiny she can't reach the upper ones without a stool. And that's not *safe.*"' Mum rolled her eyes. '"And as for your expensive rugs," I told him, "your mother's eyes are now so bad she kept on tripping on them. So they're safely rolled up in the cupboard under the stairs, taking up space that we could usefully use for her commode!" Oh, yes! I told him straight!'

I didn't want to say she almost sounded as if she was rehearsing for when Dad's pushed his luck too far. So I just asked, 'What's a commode?'

That broke the tension. Mum burst out laughing. 'Believe me, Sam. You just don't want to know!'

I thought I'd simply do what Genevieve did in the story I'd just read, and google it later. Instead, I asked, 'Was Mrs Harris's son embarrassed?'

'Him? That'll be the day! If that suspicious, meddling lump was capable of embarrassment, we'd see the man more often!'

She turned the engine on.

I asked her, partly as a joke, 'Safe to drive, are you?'

She took a deeper breath. 'I think so. Yes. I've calmed down now.' She changed the subject. 'How's the book?'

'It's fine,' I said. 'The first two stories are about boarding schools.' And then I came out with a question I'd never dared to ask before for fear of giving Mum and Dad ideas. 'Did you two never think of sending me?'

'To boarding school?'

'I know that some army people can get a grant to pay for most of it. So did you never ask?'

'No, Sam. We never asked.'

'Why not? If I'd been off at school, sometimes you could have gone abroad with Dad instead of staying home with me.'

I thought she looked a little shifty. 'I suppose I could.'

I wasn't going to let it go. 'Well, then. Why *didn't* you?'

I could see Mum was getting really uncomfortable. I thought it might be something to do with her and Dad. But as she pulled the car out into the road, she said, 'If you must know, Sam, I never thought you were the type.'

Now that was interesting – that the decision was to do with me. 'So what's "the type"?'

'Stop pestering me!' she said. 'I have to concentrate at this next roundabout. I always manage to get lost, finding the Pinkneys.'

I took the hint and reached out for my book.

Eclipse of the Sun

I dreaded changing schools. Oh, I was glad that I was starting at Carterton because it meant I'd get to go home at nights. But since it's a normal school with normal people in it I knew – just *knew* – that all day, every day, I'd get that question: 'George, what's it like to be blind?'

What is it like? I don't know. How *should* I know? I've nothing to compare it with because I have no sight at all. I never have. Most of the children back at Frith Lodge at least remembered being able to see something once, even if it was only a blur, or some kind of light. My mate Tom could see perfectly well when he was young. Then one day he saw little black things in his eyes. Then more and more black things, and his eyes frosted over. 'Just like a bathroom window,' he said (though that didn't mean a thing to me).

And then, when he was nearly blind, he came to Frith House.

If you could see a bit, then you were called a

51

partial. Me, I'm a total. I was born this way. I didn't even have proper eyes. These ones I've got are artificial, so I don't look weird. I've had nine pairs so far. Mum chose the colour – grey-green, so they'd be the same as Dad's. We have to change them regularly as my eye sockets grow. I am supposed to take my eyes out every other day to wash them in this disinfectant stuff, like contact lenses. I swallowed one of my eyes once by mistake. Dad panicked, but Mum said that all we'd have to do is wait a couple of days to get it back.

And she was right.

Sometimes I joke about putting my eyes in backwards to freak people out. But there is only one way they sit comfortably and so I can't. No one would guess that they're not real. 'You're the best-looking child I have,' Mum tells me. (But she could be lying. I am the only one who wouldn't know.)

So I got horribly nervous about the business of changing schools. Frith Lodge was closing down. The place was huge with massive grounds because in the old days there used to be so many more children who were blind and needed education. A lot of mothers used to get German measles at the exact wrong time. Some sickly new-born babies had too much oxygen pumped into their cots before the doctors realized what that did. Dozens of children had accidents with fireworks, and chemicals that had been carelessly stored before the safety people got going. Stuff like that.

And some, like me, were just born with no sight.

Frith Lodge was far too big. And finally it was agreed there weren't enough of us to make it worthwhile keeping us in one expensive building. The idea was to send us home and start us at some nearby school with loads of extra support. I knew that being with my mum and dad and brothers would make up for not being near to Tom, except online. But I had no idea how I'd fit in at Carterton High. Back at Frith Lodge I had no reason to feel out of things. We mostly all did things the same. We all played football, though the game kept having to stop for what Mr Pugh jokingly called 'bad light'. (That was whenever a train went past the playing fields. Whoever had the ball had to hang on to it, and we all stayed in place till things were quiet enough for us to hear the bell tinkling inside it again.)

In summer it was cricket. Whoever was bowling had to bounce the ball twice over if the person who was batting was a total, and once if they were a partial. It was quite big, and you could hear it rattling as it came through the air towards you.

But most of the day was lessons. Some of the teachers were blind too. They needed to know exactly where all their stuff was so they stayed in their own classrooms, and we did all the moving round. We kept to the left side of corridors. Most of the partials knew where they were just from the way the light fell. But if I wasn't paying much attention I often had to check the braille strip along the walls. Room 6. Room 8. If you weren't careful you could find yourself in the wrong class – though if you'd picked one with a blind teacher no one was likely to notice, and even you might not catch on until the lesson began.

I think the classes were like everywhere. Just endless nagging. 'Come in and sit down, please. Quickly! Millie, stop mucking about. And you too, Mandy. Quietly, please! Paper all ready in braillers? Those of you with pencils, have you got them sorted?'

On and on. I'm really good at reading braille, except for the way I slouch. ('George! Don't scrub your nose on the paper!') But it is tiresome. Everyone else can just glance at a book and know if it's the sort of thing that they might want to read. The picture on the cover says a lot. That one is scary. This one looks soppy. Here's a war story. That's a book of jokes. That has such big print it must be for babies.

We totals can't see any of that. Most of the braille books sit on the shelves in big brown rows, and you would have to pull them out and read a bit before you'd know if they were what you wanted to check out. It's easier to listen to what the others have said on the computer. (Yes, my computer talks. It has a funny little cartoon voice, and I can speed it up until it talks so fast no one but me can follow.)

The class I hated most in Frith Lodge was Life Skills, and that's because it brought it home to you that you were *different*. Some of the things you'd known since you were tiny. (Make sure your finger's in the glass before you pour, so you'll know when to stop. Put all your stuff away in the right place or you won't find it again.) My mum was using most of the tricks right from the start: 'Chips at six, George. And ketchup at nine o'clock.' (She means where it is on the plate, not when I get to eat it.)

A lot of things you learn from bitter experience (like sniffing hard at any bottle you've been given before you start to drink. No one makes that mistake twice!) But they do have to nag us all the time about some of the others. We have to be reminded not to press our eyes (the partials get good flashes) or rock in our seats like babies. (A lot of us are really bad at that.) They try to drum it into us that, even though we can't see them, people are often watching. So we must learn not to do things like scratching our bums or picking our noses without thinking first.

Some of the Life Skills stuff is supposed to be fun. We get small quizzes about things like animals and birds. If you can't see or feel the real thing, then it's hard to know how big or small they are. I spent forever just assuming owls and penguins were about the same size. And I forget which animals have tails. So all these quizzes annoy me. I hate the fact that other people just pick this stuff up without even thinking, yet I have to make a massive effort to remember it if I'm not going to sound a fool.

Yes, I hate that. I think I'd always wanted there to be at least one thing that I could do that no one else can. And I wanted it to be something real, not just a skill I've had to learn because I'm blind, like reading braille, or recognizing faces only by touch.

I wanted it to be something that came as a surprise to *everyone*.

I can't say there were any big surprises lurking at Carterton High. I'd heard a lot from my brothers, and knew the lay-out of the school from coming in for concerts and plays. My new support worker, Fay, took me in twice before the start of term so I could learn my way about while it was was quiet and calm. Mum and I met the teachers, and we discussed what I could do and what I probably couldn't, even with help from Fay.

Then it was the first day. The noise was *awful*. I expect that people stared at me as I went by. (I used my stick.) Fay chummed me to my seat. Miss Franklyn introduced me to the class. And I was one more pupil.

It didn't take that long to get used to things being different. Take the canteen. At Frith Lodge you could press a button for a speaking menu. At Carterton, I had to ask someone to read the daily list of meals to me. Not a big deal.

I wasn't teased. I think that most of them were much more curious than put off by my being in their school. They asked the usual questions. 'Do you have supersonic hearing?' And, 'Does your cat know you're blind?' That sort of thing. (No, I don't have special hearing. I simply listen more. And yes, my cat knows that I'm blind. She knows I don't know that she's there till she starts purring, or comes to be felt.)

I had to change my ways of getting about. Indoors in Frith Lodge, you held your stick across the centre of the body, only sweeping it from side to side when you were out of the house. But no one ever left things on the floor there. That was the strictest rule. At Carterton High, if I'd not swept my stick along the corridors, I would have tripped and fallen twenty times a day. School bags were left in heaps. Hockey sticks people had propped up against the walls slid down across the floor. The janitor just parked his trolley anywhere he chose.

I couldn't leave things anywhere, either.

Someone would move it and I'd end up in these stupid conversations.

'This project you've just lost – what did it look like, George?'

'A few large sheets of paper.'

'Brown or white?'

'I've no idea.'

'Oh, sorry!'

I got the work done with a bit of help. At first, the clicking of the braille machine annoyed Milusia, who sat next to me. But then she let on that that was because I went at it so fast she worried she was falling behind in taking notes. When I explained the way it works, she did cheer up a little. And she didn't mind shunting across each time Fay came to help out.

Milusia asked me once, 'What do you think I look like?'

I wondered for a moment if she was flirting. But I still answered with the truth: 'I don't think about it at all.' Because I don't. People like me don't even see in dreams. I smell and hear and feel. But I don't see.

'Well,' she said, 'I have fair hair and ice-blue eyes.'

I don't know why I was suspicious, but I asked Jason, 'Does she?'

'No.'

You'd have to be an idiot not to check, but it's

all the same to me. I don't do colours. Obviously I've learned that grass is green and sky is blue, and all that stuff. But it means nothing. You can send me to my room for my grey shirt, and I can bring it down, but that's because I know the way it feels, or how a button's hanging loose. Something like that.

I joined the chess club. Back in Frith Lodge, the white squares in our sets were sunk into the board, and the white pieces all had pointy heads. But by the time I left I could play in my head without feeling the board, so I got in the second team at Carterton quite fast, and I enjoyed that.

But I wasn't the best. No, I was never best at anything.

Until July 11th.

There had been plenty of talk of what was coming. An eclipse of the sun. For me, the moon and sun might just as well be out of fairy tales, like unicorns and dragons. How do I know they're really up there, hanging in the sky? It could be an on-going tease.

But still, Miss Jacques had given us a lesson on the way the planets move. We'd had a film, and Fay had whispered the visuals for me. I could remember when, back in my second year at Frith Lodge, we'd all been given a real planet's name, told how it spins, and guided in our separate rolling routes around the football pitch till we could do it without bumping into one another. 'That's how the planets work,' Katie had told us. 'That's how they spin across the sky in patterns.'

None of it meant much to me. I had a lot more grip on how it worked this time around, being a good deal older. But I can't say I took much interest.

As we went out through the swing doors into the fresh air, Mr Harrison gave us dark glasses. (I have my own, of course, because when I'm in places where it's too crowded for my stick, dark glasses help to warn people that I can't see.) But I was handed a cheap 'Watch the Eclipse' pair, just like everyone else. The sides were cardboard and the centre lenses felt stiff and glossy. 'Like an old photo negative,' Milusia said.

I put them on just for a laugh.

We were all led out on the playing fields. Our class stood in a line with Mr Harrison's, because Miss Franklyn was off. He spent the last few minutes giving us another lecture about keeping the glasses we'd been given on at all times. He just went on and on. And then he said it one more time, and really loudly. 'I mean it, everyone! Looking directly at the sun can burn your retina. You could be *blinded for life*.'

I *hate* moments like that. I feel as if I'm in a tank in an aquarium. I know that everyone's turning to stare at me because he's managed to make it sound as if the very worst thing in the world is being blind.

He didn't seem to notice what he'd said. He just began a sort of count down to the coming eclipse.

Then suddenly he broke off.

'Now no more talking, anyone! And that'll include me. What everyone's about to see is so special you'll remember it all of your lives.' He added threateningly, 'And there will be a serious punishment for anyone who spoils it by speaking in the next few minutes.'

They found it easier than I expected to settle down. But then again, the world did suddenly seem strange. The air around felt chillier by the minute as the moon slid across. The word 'sunless' sprang up inside my brain, and it meant far more than it had before.

The birds fell silent. That was creepy in a way. You don't expect something like that – birds noticing that something's odd about the world, and shutting up.

We stood and waited. Beside me, Cerys caught her breath.

Then, moment by moment, I could feel that the eclipse was coming to an end. A sliver of sun's warmth was reaching us again.

That's when I made myself famous. I stepped

out of line and whipped off the glasses I had been wearing only for a laugh.

I stared into the sun.

I heard the sharp intakes of breath, but no one spoke. They told me afterwards that everyone grinned and turned to see what Mr Harrison would say or do.

Milusia says he opened his mouth to yell and then broke off, as he remembered. He must have thought that I was making a fool of him. Maybe that's when he realized what he'd said about being blinded for life.

I wasn't going to step back into line in any case. I waved the cardboard glasses in the air and threw my head back with my eyes wide open. I'm told that more than one person in my class was trying not to snigger. But there were one or two who noticed nothing since they were staring up.

And the eclipse was almost over.

Even before he'd said that everyone could talk again, Mr Harrison had grasped my arm. 'Right, young man. Come along with me. We need to have a talk.'

But it was not at all what I expected. Once we were sitting in his room, he started up with an apology. 'I didn't *think*,' he told me. 'I'm really sorry about what I said. You know – "What every-one's about to *see*".'

He'd got it wrong. I use that word myself. I

always have. (My mother says when I was only three I wouldn't wear a winter hat with ear flaps. 'Take it off!' I used to shout. 'I can't *see* anything! You take it off!')

So there's no point in people choosing different words because it's me. I hate it when they say a normal thing like, 'Don't you *see*?' then rush to say they're sorry. I don't mind things like that at all.

And he was right to warn them they could blind themselves. So I felt that I should explain.

'No, it was me,' I said. 'Just for once in my whole life I wanted to show that there's one thing that I can do that no one else can.'

He burst out laughing with relief. 'And that was it?'

'Yes,' I said. 'That was it.'

He laughed some more. Then he gave me a ticking-off. 'There will be tons of better and more special things that you can do,' he said. 'Why, there's no reason on earth why someone like you can't . . .'

Bleh, bleh, bleh. I've heard that speech so often that I'm sick of it. I didn't listen.

'. . . sure you understand?' he finished up.

'Yes,' I said meekly. 'Honestly. I understand.'

It isn't true, though. Even if I become the first man in the world to fly unaided to the moon, find a quick cure for cancer and jump from the top of

Mount Everest without a parachute, all of these things will be eclipsed by that first triumph.

Nothing could ever beat standing right there in front of everyone, without dark glasses.

Staring at the sun.

Remember when you were young, and made your way around a room with your eyes closed to try to see what it would be like to be blind? Well, I did that – not going anywhere, of course, because I was in the car. But feeling in the side pockets of the door, and running my fingers over the dashboard to see what I recognized. Then I tried getting flashes, like George said the partials did, by pressing my eyeballs. Either I did it wrong or it doesn't work on people who have normal eyes.

I didn't hear Mum coming. I must have looked a little odd because she asked at once, 'Are you all right, Sam? Is it your stomach? Is it hurting again?'

I opened my eyes fast. 'No. Something in the book just set me thinking.'

'That's all right, then.' She reached behind her for the list on the back seat. 'Who's next . . . ?'

'How were the Pinkneys?' I asked, for all the world as if I knew them.

We set off towards the by-pass. 'Struggling

along,' she told me as soon as she was safely in the right-hand lane. 'He's more than halfway to gaga. Sometimes she can't handle him. And he keeps her awake, muttering and grumbling in his sleep.'

'Like Dad when he has flashbacks?'

'Nothing that bad. But all night every night, which is more tiring for his wife. The poor man thinks he's back in Leeds, running their carpet shop.' She gave herself a little shake. 'I tell you, Sam, on days like these, I start to dread old age.'

'It doesn't sound like a cakewalk.'

She made a face. 'That's an odd, old-fashioned way of putting it.'

I tapped *Away From Home*. 'It comes up in this book.' And that reminded me. 'You know what you were saying about me not being "the type" to go to boarding school . . .'

She wasn't having any of it, I could tell. She interrupted me. 'Sam, can you look up the next place for me on the map?'

'Why don't we get the Satnav fixed?' I asked. 'It hasn't worked for five weeks now. If we don't get it sorted, or buy another, we still won't have one by the time that Dad comes home.'

She knew exactly what I meant. Dad *hates* things that don't work. Her face went tight, but all she said was, 'Look up Delaware Road please, Sam. It's around here somewhere.' Then, while I was still running my finger down the street names in the index, she asked me, 'Are you getting hungry yet?'

I thought after my claims of stomach ache it might be wiser to pretend not to be starving for a little longer. 'Not really, no. But I think that I might be soon.'

'All right,' she said. 'We'll pick up something after I've done the twins.'

'The twins?'

'Moira and Marcia Fletcher.'

'How old are they?'

'I'm not sure. In their early nineties, I suppose.'

It would have sounded stupid to say to her, 'And they're still twins?' But that was in my mind. I suppose I always think of twins as babies, or people in school.

'Do they still look alike?'

'Totally.'

They did, too. When we pulled up outside their house, we saw them standing side by side beside their garage looking exactly like one of those Spot the Difference drawings. The only difference I could see was that one held a hoe, the other a rake.

'They still do their own *gardening*?'

'You don't stay upright that old, sitting on your bum,' said Mum, and left me to watch her herding the two ancient ladies back in their house.

Only after the door had closed behind them did I pick up the book again.

Folie à Deux

That's French. It means a madness shared by two, and I was in one once. This was light years ago, when I was a small boy in knee pants, back in that hateful prep school. You can't imagine how bad things were at boarding schools back then.

Winters were worst, of course. Jack Frost ice patterns on the insides of the dormitory windows. The toothpaste frozen in the tubes. The floors so cold our feet almost stuck to them. The water in the showers chilly beyond belief, and if you didn't step right under it, you'd get a black mark.

Five black marks and you'd earned a beating.

Oh, yes. They beat us. Mr Philips did it with a cane. We queued up once a week to get our punishments.

'How many, Rutherfield?' (Like every other pupil, I had left my Christian name at home, along with my dog and teddy bear. If you had brothers, the teachers added a number onto the end of your surname to keep things straight for them: Scott-Freeman I, Scott-Freeman II, and then the twins, Scott-Freemen III and IV. Like cogs in a machine.)

'Come on, boy. Don't waste my time. How many strokes?'

'Four please, Sir.'

'Right you are.'

His strokes did hurt. But not as much as those of other masters. (None of the women who taught us ever touched a cane. They left it to the men to do the job.)

The teachers kept us busy all day long. They took it as a failure on their part to catch you doing nothing. 'Wasting time, Harding? Go and ask Matron for a bucket and mop, and clean this corridor. Right now!'

Even our daily walks could be a misery if it was your turn at the front. They'd turn into another lesson, with the teacher glancing left or right, then going on about water tables and springs, or contour lines, or trees misshapen by the prevailing wind.

And we were hungry. All the time. Tea was the only meal where you could eat until you'd had enough. To this day I can't look at margarine without repulsion. Once Lucan II did an experiment. He filched a teaspoonful of every single thing they gave us to eat in one week, including margarine. He put the samples into upturned bottle tops and spread them out along an unused shelf in one of the gardener's tumble-down sheds.

We all trooped in to take a look. And then we left them.

After a week we went back and everything was gone except the margarine. That just sat where we had left it in its bottle top, unlicked, untouched.

'See? Unfit to eat. Not even insects want it.'

'Not even rats or woodlice.'

'Probably *poisonous.*'

But it was the only thing that made the curling edges of the bread go down. So we still ate it.

Then, one day, a new boy came. His name was Quentin. (Rupert Allinson Quentin was the name burned on his banded trunk.) He had black hair and sharp blue eyes that darted round the room, then settled suddenly on me.

I felt the strangest shiver.

Our form master, Mr Leroy, glanced around the room to find a desk for Quentin. I sat by Binfield then, tight in the corner. On the far side there was a spare desk next to Lucan II, and Mr Leroy was clearly just about to lift his hand to point to it. He even opened his mouth to say to Quentin, 'You can take that seat.'

But nothing happened. Not a word came out and Mr Leroy's hand stayed where it was.

Quentin had turned his clear blue eyes directly onto him.

There was a moment's silence, as if the world had suddenly stopped in its tracks. Then Mr Leroy said, 'Binfield, pack up your stuff and move across to sit by Lucan II. Quentin, you take that seat beside Rutherfield.'

And Quentin smiled. It wasn't any friendly, I-hope-I'm-going-to-like-you smile. It was a smirk of triumph, as if to let me know that he had wanted to sit in my corner and he'd got his way.

I knew at once that Quentin was a sorceror. I never doubted from the start that he could make things happen. I wasn't frightened. Hadn't he looked around the class and chosen me?

I was excited.

We kept our heads down until break, and I could tell that Quentin had no trouble with the work. He never seemed to turn to look at what I wrote, but once or twice his hand would stray across to my side of the double desk and tap the page. I'd look towards him but he would be facing the other way. So I'd look down to see where he was pointing and, unerringly, he'd found a word spelled wrong or a misplaced apostrophe for me to correct.

That was the first time in my life I got full marks for anything I wrote.

When the bell rang for break and we had been dismissed, he turned his eyes on me. 'Ready?'

I didn't ask 'for what?' I simply nodded. Not even bothering to stop at Binfield's desk to say I hadn't wanted him to have to move, I followed Quentin from the room.

He led me down the path towards the shrubbery as confidently as if he was the one who'd been at the school for years and I was the boy who'd started only that morning. We reached the greenhouse by the vegetable garden wall.

I panicked. 'But we're not allowed down here.'

'It'll be fine. The gardener's not around.'

I didn't even wonder how he knew. I just believed him. From that first day I took as gospel every word that Quentin said. I didn't criticize what he was saying, either. If anyone else had sat perched on that water barrel talking about their 'high-born' family, I would have hated listening. Boasting in our school was an absolute sin. But every word that Quentin said was magical to me. He told me all about the way his ancestors had helped Queen Mary with some important treaty or another, and how in gratitude she'd granted them their fine estates. He talked of great alliances, and how the most noble blood ran through his family from splendid marriages on either side.

He told me that his grandmother had been a witch. He had inherited the gift of second sight. He could cast spells.

73

'What?' I remember asking. '*Real* spells?'

'Yes. Real spells.'

I heard the first bell ring. 'We must get back.'

'You go,' he said. 'I might stay here for a while.'

Quite terrified at the idea, I said, 'You can't be late for lessons – no, not here.'

He looked contemptuous. 'I can do what I like.'

I started arguing, but he turned away. Losing my nerve, I ran back to the school. I made a wrong turn in the shrubbery out of pure panic and came in through the western door. I ran through the cloakrooms, up the stairs and past the Junior Sports notice board, into our classroom.

There he was, sitting calmly at his desk. As I skidded to a halt, he raised his head and smiled.

I was so shaken. How had he managed it? There was another way into the school. But still, I'd left him trailing his finger idly in the water butt. And here he was back in his seat, not even panting.

Not even looking flushed.

That afternoon I asked about his handwriting. It was so spidery, with odd little curlicues on top of some of his letters.

'That is because I mostly write in Persian,' he explained.

'Persian?'

'Yes. It's the best language for writing spells.'

I was dumbstruck. The only thing that I could think to say was, 'Can I see what it looks like?'

'Persian writing?'

'Yes.'

He gave a doubtful look. 'But then you'd have to see my Book of Spells.'

'You have a book of them?'

'Of course.'

That night, he showed me. While everyone was busy milling around the dormitory, making the most of the free hour before bed, he touched my arm. 'Coming?'

He held a burlap bag, as if the two of us were going shopping. Curious, I let him lead me out and up the stairs to the night lavatories. 'There,' he said, drawing out of his bag what he'd been hiding. 'This is my Book of Spells.'

It looked to me as if it had been made by hand out of some sort of parchment. The edges were ragged. Around the stained and wrinkled cover were oriental patterns, so intricately inked in places that they were almost solid black. Across the front, painted in faded silver, was strange, indecipherable lettering.

'Go on,' he said. 'Open it up and look.'

I can't describe the inside properly, except to say it looked a little like my father's scrap book of pressed flowers. But where my father simply wrote in the name of every flower, the spell book was entirely filled with spidery foreign writing. Odd things were tucked between the pages. There was a tiny fan of seven different lengths of flattened straw, and small pools of coloured sand glued to a double page. A strip of what looked like shrivelled lizard skin was pinned in one place, and a dried leaf stuck to another. Between the next two pages, crumbling shards of bark were wedged close to the book's fat spine.

As each page turned, the book gave off hot spicy smells that made me think of the bazaars I'd read about in *The Arabian Nights*.

'Can we try one tomorrow?'

'A spell? They're not for *fun*.'

The way he said it made me feel as if I had been childish. To try to cover my tracks, I said, 'There must be *something* that you want. Or don't want.'

He gave me a strange look. 'I expect there is,' he said. 'And when we come across it, I shall show you.'

And then, just as if Quentin and I were in a play on stage and our scene was over, there was frantic rattling at the door. I looked across to see the handle twisting back and forth.

After a moment I heard Binfield's voice. 'Open up! I need to get in there.'

'The door's not locked,' called Quentin.

'Yes, it—'

The voice broke off as Binfield almost fell into the room. He looked quite startled to see us standing so far away, under the frosted window. 'I was sure it was locked.'

'No,' Quentin told him easily.

'It *felt* locked.'

Quentin just smiled and pushed his Book of Spells back in the burlap bag. I could tell Binfield was curious about what we'd been doing. But he was desperate for the lavatory, and hurried to the nearest cubicle. I still felt bad about the fact that we'd been separated in class, and being found with Quentin made it worse. So after Quentin left, I hung around till Binfield emerged.

'Your new friend?' he said, somewhat scathingly.

I felt my colour rise. 'I didn't ask for him to be put next to me.'

'You should be careful,' Binfield warned. 'Scott-Freeman has been telling us about the family. It seems that Quentin was kicked out of his last school.'

'Kicked out? But why?'

I could tell Binfield was more thrilled with what he had to tell than he was letting on. 'This awful thing happened. Some boy sleepwalked his way out of the main school and over the courtyard in the middle of the night. He some-how made his way through a locked chapel door, went up a spiral stair and out onto the roof. Then he stepped off.'

'Stepped off the *roof*?'

Binfield's hand made the gesture of something falling. Hard. 'And he was killed.'

'They didn't think that Quentin pushed him!'

'No, no. Nothing like that. It seems that everyone was woken by the scream, and Quentin was right there in bed, like everyone else.'

I thought about the piercing look Quentin had given Mr Leroy. Then of a boy's broken body, sprawled across stone cobbles. 'So Quentin *couldn't* have done it,' I tried to reassure myself.

'No,' Binfield said. 'But he did say that it was going to happen.'

'*What*?'

Binfield repeated himself. 'The night before, he'd told the other boys that it was going to happen.'

It seemed impossible – the sort of story you'd make up to give the other people in your dorm night shivers. 'How does Scotty *know* all this?'

'Because his father is a barrister. There was a court case. The dead boy's parents claimed that since Rupert Quentin had described the fall before it even happened, he must have had something to do with it.'

'He really did tell people? *Before*?'

'He said he'd seen it in his magic mirror.'

'There's no such thing.'

'I know that. But that's what he said, and so the parents said it must be sorcery and started a court case. Mr Scott-Freeman knows the barrister that Quentin's mother hired for the defence. He said that Quentin's family would have won in any event because there's no such thing as magic and the accusations were "downright absurd". But, as it happened, the other boy's family lost the case for quite another reason . . .'

I felt a chill even before Binfield came out with it.

'Their barrister dropped dead. That very morning. His young assistant did his best, but made a hash of it – though Scotty's father insists they would have lost the case anyway since nobody in their right mind believes in magic mirrors.'

I caught at Binfield's sleeve. 'But is that really what Quentin told them? Under a solemn oath? That he saw everything in some weird mirror?'

'Nobody *let* him say it. Quentin was not allowed to open his mouth in court.' Binfield grinned. 'And I bet I know why! Quentin's so creepy he could probably persuade the jury that he truly had seen what he said.'

I've no idea what made me say it, but I did. 'Perhaps he *did* see something.'

Binfield gave me the oddest look. And then he grinned, and laid the tips of his fingers on my forehead. 'Yeeouch!' he said, snatching his hand back as if my skin was hot enough to scorch him. 'You must be feverish even to *say* that!'

I pummelled him in the old way as we went down the stairs.

That night I had the strangest dreams. Time and again, convinced that Rupert Quentin must be standing right beside my bed, I'd snap my eyes open to find no one there. I'd close my eyes again, and back the image of him came, so clearly I was sure it must be real.

By morning, I was twitching tired. He told me, 'You look terrible,' then smiled. 'Didn't you sleep?'

It sounded just a bit too much like mockery, and I made up my mind to spend as little time with him as possible. I planned to sit with my old friends at breakfast time, and I decided that each time a bell rang to signal the end of class I'd rush across the room to see what Binfield and his mates were doing. Then I'd go off with them.

It didn't work that way. Somehow that morning Quentin managed to attach himself to every group I joined. His presence seemed to make them uneasy. One by one, they'd melt away on some excuse.

'Just got to fetch a book.'

'Oh, I forgot. I said to Scotty that I'd find some dice for him.'

'I'm meeting Winthrop in the library.'

Soon, only Binfield was left. Quentin turned his way, and within moments, as if in a trance, Binfield went off without a word.

There was a satisfied look on Quentin's face. 'Coming?'

I fell in step with him. Inside my head I was remembering a passage of the Bible I'd been made to learn as punishment for talking in chapel: 'Whither thou goest, I shall go . . .'

It seemed to *matter*.

Still, I couldn't think of any reason not to follow him. It's not as if we did much – unless you count as worthwhile sitting listening to someone bragging. We got into the habit of wandering down to one of the abandoned dens in the shubbery. There, Quentin would talk about how brilliant he was at some old Chinese game I'd never heard of in my life. He said that he could speak in Ancient Assyrian. He told me that his father handed him a gun once when the two of them were on safari, and he had shot a tiger. He claimed to know half of the Spanish royal family. He even claimed that he could understand the language of animals, and often advised the local vet at home because he could explain where their pains were.

I never even scoffed! I just sat there and listened avidly, for all the world as if he'd put me, Louis Rutherfield, under one of his own spells.

When I was with him, everyone avoided me.

Sometimes, if old friends passed me on a stair-case or in the lavatories, they might break step and mutter, 'How can you spend so much time with him? He gives me the *creeps*.' Or, 'Can you really like him? He's so *peculiar*.' I don't know why, but their dislike of my new friend meant almost nothing to me. I was in thrall to Quentin. Something about the way he talked, the things he said, held me entirely captive.

Then somebody I hardly knew said nastily one morning, 'And how is Quentin's little lapdog today?'

The sheer contempt in his voice got through to me. I felt a wash of shame and told myself I would stand up to Quentin more.

That afternoon it poured with rain. There was no going out. With all his usual confidence, he said, 'We'll go along the kitchen corridor. It'll be warmer there.'

'No,' I said. 'Let's look in your magic mirror.'

I'd hoped to startle him into seeing me as something other than his slave and toady. I thought he'd turn to stare and ask, 'How do you know about *that*?'

The question never came. Still, I was nervous enough to burst out with the explanation any-way: 'Scotty told us about the court case.'

'Scott-Freeman II should be careful,' Quentin said.

Then, as if the conversation never happened

and the words I'd said had simply been an idle wind that had blown past, he took off for the kitchen corridor.

I tried my very hardest not to follow him.

It can't have been more than a couple of days before I saw Binfield racing down the main staircase towards me. 'Ruthers! Guess what! I've just been in the dorm. Quentin's up there. I saw him staring in this little mirror so I crept up behind him – just to tease, you understand.'

'Tease?'

'Make a joke – you know – about him primping in mirrors!' He dropped his voice conspiratorially. 'When I got close enough I loomed up over his shoulder. I thought he'd see my face in the reflection and drop the mirror in fright. But it was really *weird*. I'll tell you what I saw. It was—'

He broke off, staring into space.

'Binny? What did you see? What was there in the mirror?'

Still Binfield was silent. All he did was stare ahead vacantly, his mouth still open.

'Binny? Binfield!'

But there was no response. It was as if he had been changed into a statue on the spot.

'Binny!'

Then he came back to life. 'What?'

'What did you see in the mirror?'

'Mirror?'

'The mirror you were telling me about. The one Quentin was holding.'

'Quentin? I've not seen him all day, except in class. You are the one who spends all his time with Quentin.'

And with a bound onto the parquet flooring of the hall, Binfield was off.

I hoped it was a tease, and waited till evening, when I could catch Binfield alone. I asked him once again about the mirror, and this time he even seemed to have forgotten that we'd met on the stairs. He gave me the strangest look, as if he thought that there was something wrong with me.

So I gave up. But I was terrified. What had he seen? And why had Quentin wiped it from his brain before he could tell me? I went up to the dorm and tried to act as if nothing had happened. But I was now convinced I'd crossed some sort of line with Quentin. It had been the worst mistake to let him know I'd heard about the court case and the magic mirror. Quentin had uncanny powers. And he could be malignant. I lay there worrying that I would be the next to sleepwalk off a tower and crash onto the stones below.

That night I couldn't sleep for fear that, when I opened my eyes, I'd see him watching me. I spent the hours watching the shadows of the dormitory take on strange shapes, and hearing threats in almost every sleeping breath drawn by the boys around me.

Just before dawn I saw him coming, sliding silently across the floor as if on oiled wheels. He held a little mirror out towards my face, and he was smiling, smiling.

Even while I was screaming, he still smiled.

I had to leave. My parents were informed it was a *folie à deux*. 'Shared madness,' said the doctor. 'It seems this Rupert Quentin is convinced that he has magic powers, and your son's fallen in with this belief and spooked himself out of his wits. He would be better off away from here, till he recovers.'

My father brought me home. My mother took one look at my pale face and shivering limbs, and told him firmly that she would not let me out of her sight till I was myself again.

And so we walked along to my old Dame School after the younger children had gone home, and I took lessons once again with Mrs Braithwaite. She was so kind – oh, everyone was kind. But nothing did so much to heal my mind as getting the hurried letter from Binfield telling me that Rupert Quentin had left the school for good.

'Kicked out again. So you can come back, Ruthers.'

There'd been an accident. I didn't piece the story together till later. All I knew was that our Scott-Freeman somehow found a way out of the school at night, and wandered down to the back-water, half a mile away. But for a poacher who chanced to see him striding, wide-eyed, into the reedy swamp, poor Scotty would have drowned.

After, Mr Scott-Freeman strode into our Headmaster's room and told him, 'Either that Quentin boy goes, or all four of my sons leave this school at once.'

So I was not the only one to worry about sorcery. Perhaps it wasn't a *folie à deux* at all.

Perhaps it was a *folie à trois*.

As soon as we'd chosen a table in the cafe and unloaded our tray, I said to Mum, 'Come on. Stop fudging. I only ask you a serious question once in a blue moon. It's only fair you answer. What did you mean when you said I was not the type to go to boarding school?'

She tried to shrug it off. 'Oh, nothing much. It's just that I don't think of you as someone who would take to being away from home like a duck takes to water.'

I thought about the boy in the first story who'd had to go home after only four weeks. 'You think of me as *weepy*?'

'Of course not. Nothing to do with whether you're robust or not. I'm sure you could ride over anything that came along. It's something else.'

I ate more cake. 'All right, then. Nothing to do

with being weepy. Or robust. Still, you think I'm not the type?'

She grinned. 'Well, look at you! Your age, and you still need the odd blue moon day to get you through the school year.'

'This isn't a blue moon day!'

'No? Then how come you and your terrible stomach ache have managed to demolish that huge slice of cake before I've even started on my buttered scone?'

I looked at the crumbs on my plate. 'Well, I feel better now.'

'I bet you do.' She took a sip of coffee then told me, 'All I meant was that I'm not sure it would be good for you to be with others every hour of every day. I think I would prefer to know that you have time to yourself.'

'Is that just me? Or do you think that about everyone?'

Now she was getting cagey. 'Well, of course, people come out of different boxes.' She waved a hand. 'Take the twins . . .'

'That pair you just visited?'

'Moira and Marcia, yes. They've shared a home all their lives. I once asked if either of them ever married, and they were really tickled at the notion that they might ever have wanted to live apart. But there is nothing wrong with them. They're perfectly normal.'

'I'm not so sure. Maybe they have a folie a deux.'

'*Folie a deux?*'

'It's French,' I told her, 'and it means a madness shared by two.'

'For heaven's sake!' said Mum. 'Where do you pick up all this stuff?'

I waved *Away From Home* at her. She looked a bit startled, but all she said was, 'Well, you're quite wrong. The Fletcher twins aren't mad. They're just a little different in their own way.'

I was still thinking of the boy in the first story. 'You say I'm not the type. But I bet there are loads of people sent away to school who aren't the type either.'

'Loads. And they are even more unlucky if they don't realize it.' She checked the time. 'Eat up. We're falling behind. Old people really fuss if you don't show up promptly.'

'My plate is empty,' I reminded her. 'You are the one who hasn't started yet.'

Mum ate her scone on the walk back to the car. I brushed crumbs off her as she drove towards her next appointment.

Then I picked up my book.

Dream Cell

Usually, when they throw me in the slammer, I play Dead Fish. That freaks them out.

Miss Connor used to make us play it back in nursery when we got over-excited. She'd tell us all to fetch our resting mats and spread them around the room.

'Right now. Everyone lie on your mat and wriggle like mad. Go on. Shake all those fidgets out of you.'

As soon as she had seen we'd had enough, she'd say, 'Now everyone lie still. Close your eyes. Lie there so quietly that, if you were in bed, your mum or dad would think you were asleep.'

So we'd lie there, as still as fallen statues. As soon as someone sneezed, or rubbed their nose, or shifted on the mat, Miss Connor would call out their name and they would have to tiptoe between the rest of us, to sit in a line beside her on the bright red bench.

She didn't tell us that the game was called

Dead Fish. I suppose she reckoned that might frighten us, since we were only four. She called it 'Wriggle Time'. (How wet is that?)

But I got really, really good at it. And I still am. So now, whenever the staff have shoved me into one of the isolation cells for causing trouble, I lie on the bed and play the game on my own. I can lie there, unmoving, for hours and hours, and I can tell exactly how worried they're getting from noticing how often they slide back the peep grille, and how long they leave it open, peering in.

Oh, they know perfectly well that lying there dead still is what I do. But I can almost hear them thinking, 'Perhaps it is . . . But maybe *this* time . . .' After all, I might have swallowed something dangerous, or had a seizure. My track record of behaviour isn't brilliant, but it wouldn't look so good on theirs if, when they finally panicked and took a proper look, the doctor said that I'd been dead for hours.

So even if they chance it and don't come in to shake me, I know I've rattled them a bit and even, with a bit of luck, spoiled their coffee break.

Today I'm in the cell for acting up. ('Non-compliance', they call it.) You see, those of us who are still under school-leaving age have to have lessons. Most of the classes are just another way of wasting time, but some aren't so bad, and I like almost everything we do with Miss Abbott.

She comes in every Tuesday and Thursday for something she calls Modern Studies. That sounds quite heavy, but she always manages to make whatever we're doing interesting somehow.

And now and then, like yesterday, it's even a good laugh. She made us push four of the tables together, then spread a giant sheet of clean white paper over them.

'I want you to design your own Dream City.'

Dream City. What a magic idea!

Togs started off. He chose a football stadium. We all fell in with that and we agreed it should go in the middle of the city as a sort of focal point. There was a scrap about whose was to be the home team. Voices were raised. But Miss Abbott put a stop to that by saying it would have to be the home pitch of an imaginary team. Suggested names by Thursday. Her choice of winner. (No discussion.) And there's a prize.

Her prizes are a big box of Maltesers. And you don't have to share. So we stopped arguing.

Then Sundeep said he'd want a mosque. (Of course.)

That irritated Terry. He cannot stand Sundeep. So he came back at once with the suggestion of a massive Catholic cathedral. I reckoned things were getting *bleh*, so I suggested there should be a dog track and a boxing club, and loads and loads of night clubs and pubs.

'For heaven's sake!' said Miss Abbott. 'I did

this with another group only a while ago, and their suggestions couldn't have been more different.'

'What did *they* want?'

She waved her hands about. 'Nice things. You know. Things that make up a pleasant community, like trees and parks, museums and art galleries.'

'Oh, yes,' said Terry, grinning. 'Nice things. Nursery schools and animal sanctuaries. Fancy retirement homes. Shops selling really posh clothes.'

'No thanks,' I said. 'Let's have a nuclear power station. A really badly designed one, already leaking badly and just about ready to blow.'

Miss Abbott sighed and handed out the thick black charcoal and the coloured chalks.

We set off, drawing all the things we wanted. Everyone needed a bit of elbow room around the table, so I think that we spread things too much around the edge. Certainly our Dream City's road system fetched up a right spaghetti mess, with roundabouts all over.

'Just like home,' Sundeep said. (He comes from Milton Keynes.)

'Can there be sea?' asked Pete. 'We went to some beach once when I was fostered and I thought it was fantastic.'

'Nudie beach! Nudie beach!' shouted Joel, till Red O'Reilly who was on duty at the back sloped up to lay a hand on his shoulder to calm him. 'Enough noise, lad. Miss Abbott can't hear herself speak.'

She wasn't trying. One of Pete's problems is that his hand's bandaged so bulkily from his last fight that he can't hold a pencil. So she was busy drawing a thick blue coast line down the side of our Dream City to keep him happy.

The thought of nudie beaches had set Terry off. 'And we could have a Love Motel!' (He said it in that drawling American way that comes out 'Lurve'.)

Sundeep gave him a push. 'Don't be disgusting.'

To keep the two of them from kicking off, I asked Miss Abbott, 'If it's our *perfect* city, can we have other things? Like weekends that last longer than usual?'

The idea caught on. 'And shorter mornings? Especially if it's a day for lessons.'

'And longer nights! Especially if we're in the Lurve Motel!'

We can't talk sleaze in front of staff – not even as a joke. O'Reilly casually hitched up his belt so his keys jangled. That counts as our first warning. But at the same time he was soothing things with one of his dry remarks. 'Why bother simply tinkering round the edges, lads? Why not just put the whole of your Dream City onto a teenage time zone?'

Miss Abbott played the straight man. 'How would that work, Mr O'Reilly?'

'You know. Everyone stopping up till daft o'clock, and only getting dressed in time for lunch.'

Only the crawlers grinned. I mean, O'Reilly's own teenage sons might get the chance to stay up till all hours, then lie in bed all morning. We are locked down by seven at night, and the first bell's at ten past six each morning.

Nothing funny about that.

'Right,' said Miss Abbott. 'Let's get on.'

So off we went, fitting in all the other things we'd like to have in our dream city. A skate park. Practice goalposts. Even an ice rink. (Fat chance. Most of us come from towns where the shop windows are grated up and you're not safe on the streets for druggies, loonies with knives, and car thieves screeching round corners. Jason says his aunt claims that he had never spent a single hour off their rubbish estate until some woman from the council came round to threaten Jason's mum that he'd be taken into care unless she let him go to nursery. He can remember being startled by the feel of grass under his bum. Till then, it seems, he'd only ever been strapped in his pushchair, or left to play on the cracked tarmac outside their tower block.

But he's not all that special. We are what Red O'Reilly calls 'a right sad lot'. He can't believe that half the boys on our wing can't make a cup of tea, or use a vacuum cleaner. (He finds that out by sitting in on our Life Skills class.) Some of the boys can't write their names or count their change. The teachers have a go at bolstering them up. 'If you were that damn thick, you'd still be safe at home, helping your mum. Lads who end up in here are short on *sense*, not brains. So just get on with it and finish the page.'

A lot of the time it works. Terry came in here seven months ago not even able to recognize his own name written down, let alone write it. Now he's the pride of Mr Hall, who runs the library. And I've improved a lot because they let me read and write what I want.

And draw. I've always liked that best. And that's why, while the rest of them were quarrelling about whether our dream city's swimming pool (along with flumes and waves) ought to be near the sea or on the other side of town, I was pocketing charcoal and chalks. You have to watch it when you're nicking stuff inside this place. You do have pockets, but the seams collapse. My cousin told me why. 'Too many boys kick off,' he said. 'They get shoved into isolation to cool down, and since there's nothing there to damage, they rip their clothes to shreds.'

So it turns out that what we wear is sewn with really weak thread. The stitching is so loose that any part you tug at comes apart almost at once.

Your gear looks like torn rags when thrown around the cell, but you've been fooled. Mrs Patel can sew the seams back up as good as new (by that, of course, I mean as weak and loose as new) in pretty well no time at all.

Then the next sinner gets them.

So I was careful not to stuff everything I nicked into one pocket in case I lost the lot. I spread the chalks out, and I kept a couple tucked behind the band of my trousers. I even stuck a few short stubs of charcoal in my hair. (O'Reilly calls it 'thatch', but I had no idea what he was on about until I saw a picture of a country cottage in one of the readers I was going through with Mr Hall.)

I knew they'd notice if the art supplies were thinner on the ground after we'd gone, so I made sure I was first out after the lesson ended. I was quite lucky, really. Sports had been cancelled because they were short of staff with one or two baddies more than usual being on lock-down. So we got sent back to our cells until the midday bell.

I came out with my pockets empty, and the day rolled on.

I try not to cause trouble all the time because we work on coloured cards, just like a footballer. Three yellow cards and they take all of your electrical stuff out of your room. Two red cards and you lose anything with batteries. (You're not allowed new stuff that might get a signal.) If you behave they give you points, and once you've got to silver, then you can have a telly in your room. If you're on silver for two weeks without a break, they move you to another wing.

Staff call it 'Liberty Hall'. That is a joke. But it is brilliant. I've been there twice. There is a telly lounge, and a big room with table tennis and pool. Lock down is an hour later and you can wear your own home clothes. For many of the boys it's actually better than home, and I've known more than one act up in their last week to lose remission. That way they get to stay in here another month or two – a couple of weeks back on our wing, earning their silver points, and then the last few in the lap of luxury.

I'm not like that. I hate being away from home and hope I shan't come here again.

But I was in a weird mood. I admit it. I knew right from the start why I had filched the chalks. I had a plan.

It was Miss Abbott's fault – all that talk of a Dream City. Suddenly I'd had my own idea.

My own Dream Cell.

Lock down, I told you, was at seven o'clock. The lights, though, never go out – well, not completely. So I did the bed trick. I took the stupid dolly thing my sister brought me. ('His name's Fat Gordon, and I got him for you because his hair's tufty, like yours! *And* the same colour!') I shoved

Fat Gordon under the covers. (He's been slit open, x-rayed, sniffed by dogs, and tested with a swab. Stuffed toys like him are totally against the rules in case they're stuffed with other things than fluff. The officers only didn't throw him in the bin because he came from Hetty, and she's become a pet in Family Visiting.) I tried to throw Fat Gordon out once, but Mr McFee carried him back and ticked me off royally. 'How could you, laddie! It's bad enough your not being home with your wee poppet of a sister. So don't you even *think* of tossing her lovely present to you out again!'

But finally Fat Gordon was useful, rather than a real embarrassment. He took my place in bed while I started drawing on the wall behind the cell door where I wouldn't be seen.

First I drew what I'd love most in my cell – my dream machine – a brilliant old-fashioned sound system like the one my third stepdad had before it got nicked. I drew it in black charcoal, with silver knobs for volume and tuning and balance. I drew the speakers – really big ones that would give good thrum. I drew a pile of CDs loose over the floor, just like at home, beside a classy rack with even more.

That took until I heard the warder doing his first round of peep-hole checks. As soon as he'd shot the flap closed again, I moved to the only wall that stays quite shadowy. On it I drew a dart

100

board with a treble nineteen, treble twenty and a bull's-eye, and my latest stepdad's guitar leaning against the wall beneath it. I drew a peg stand, with my precious Tottenham strips dangling. And, beside that, a poster of their new striker doing one of his brilliant flying kicks.

I drew the fixture list right next to that.

Then I crouched down because I heard more footsteps ringing down the corridor, but no one checked on me. The moment the noise was gone, I went across the cell and drew a window with a forest view, two seriously twisted window bars, and just a shred or two of Young Offenders Unit pyjamas, to show the officers how I'd escaped.

I hadn't used much of the red or yellow or the orange, so I spent half an hour drawing a massive bowl of jelly babies in all sorts of colours. Under that, I drew some magazines and comics.

Then I went back to bed. As soon as I had pushed Fat Gordon aside and got myself warm again, I realized I'd forgotten to draw food. So I got up again and drew a table with a steaming plate of chicken tikka and some poppadoms. I used up the last of the white chalk drawing tons of cucumber raitha – I can eat mountains of that – and the last of the orange chalk I'd snaffled was used up colouring in several bottles of Hetty's favourite mandarin fizz.

Then I went back to bed and slept till morning.

* * *

That's why I'm in the isolation unit now, playing Dead Fish. There's nothing else to do. I suppose that, by the time they let me out, later today, someone will have washed off my art-work.

But it was worth it. Even if they take off my remission, and Hetty has to wait a few more days to get me back, she'll understand. It was a major laugh. The warders all came in to take a look. Red O'Reilly even took photos. ('You've got real talent there, lad. I'm going to bring you in a print-out of my photographs of these four walls so you can go for an apprenticeship when you get out. I should think any signwriter in your home town would want to snap you up.')

The peep-hole's being slid back every couple of minutes now. They're getting anxious. Sooner or later, one of them will crack and open up to give me a good shake or tickle, until I crack and grin.

They'll say exactly what they always say. 'Next time we shan't come in until we see your body rotting.'

I've thirty-eight more days to go. You have to pass them *somehow*.

When Mum came back, she passed the map across. 'I need a bit of help to get to this next appointment.'

It just popped out. 'I *told* you that we ought to get the Satnav fixed.'

Mum raised an eyebrow. Had she realized that I was getting tense? Sometimes Dad doesn't let us know his travel plans. Often he doesn't know them because they're what he calls 'pillar to post'. Sometimes he does, and then we go to pick him up. I could already picture him flinging his massive pack into the back of the car and falling, exhausted, into the seat beside Mum, but instantly noticing the dead face of the Satnav. '*It's still not working, then? You didn't think to get it fixed all the time I was away?*'

It's always something like that. Some little niggle that will spoil the mood.

Mum knows that, too, but all she said to me was, 'Well, I do remember that we start by going through four roundabouts in a row.'

I tried to brush my worries away. 'Four? It's like Milton Keynes.'

She gave me quite a look. 'When have you ever been to Milton Keynes?'

'I haven't. I just know there are a lot of round-abouts.' I waved *Away From Home* at her.

'This book is getting to sound more and more odd.' She slid the car in gear. 'Now don't forget to count.'

'One!' I said. Then, because the next roundabout wasn't even in sight, I took the chance to remind her, 'Back in the cafe you said that someone who had gone away to school would be unlucky if they hadn't realized they weren't the type.'

'I think so, yes. They might think that there was something *wrong* with them when all the time there wasn't.'

'Suppose you were sent to prison.' I clocked the second roundabout. 'That's number two. One of those prisons for young people.'

'You mean a secure unit?'

'I suppose so. Then you would know you *couldn't* leave, and that was that. So you would actually be better off than someone in a boarding school who hadn't realized it was wrong for them. This roundabout that's coming up is number three.'

'I suppose you would.' Mum braked for a woman trying to kill herself crossing the road. 'Though I suppose that having been to boarding school might turn out useful later. It's said that people who were sent away to school settle down fast in jail.'

'And prisoner-of-war camps. This one is number four. You turn left here. People from boarding schools get on really well in prisoner-of-war camps too.'

'How do you know all this?'

I tapped *Away From Home*.

'Good job you brought that with you,' she declared as we pulled into a neat private carpark ringed by shrubbery. 'This next one might take quite a time. Miss Shefford's very deaf. I have to bellow everything at least four times.'

'Why can't she get a better hearing aid?'

Mum switched the engine off and gave me a long look. 'Oh, Sam,' she said. 'You have a lot to learn about the horrors of the failing body. So try and make the most of being fit and young.'

And then she left.

Last One Picked

Lop. That's what they call me. When I arrived at Leeside from my old school, I had no nickname at all. In fact, after a couple of weeks here I'd begun to feel as if I hadn't even kept my real name. Whole days would pass with no one saying 'Daniel'. The teachers rarely called on me to go on errands, or answer questions in class, and everyone in my year group had their own friends. I think I might have stayed invisible, except that we play lots of games and I kept dropping things. They would all roll their eyes and groan, especially if it meant we lost the match, or fluffed the chance at a goal.

That's when they started to call me Lop. (It stands for Last One Picked.)

I haven't told my mother. She'd get so upset. She only wanted me to come to Leeside so I would not be teased, like in my old school. I think she must have thought that children who had parents rich enough to pay school fees would probably be kinder.

And things *are* better here. In my old school you could be bullied and even some of the grown-ups on the staff would pretend not to notice. Here at least I'm lucky enough to have Gervaise in my class, and he sticks up for me.

'Don't pick on poor old Lop. He can't help being clumsy.'

'Why are you bowling like *that*? You know Lop can't hit balls that come so fast.'

'At least Lop's problem has a proper name. It's in the medical books. But you're just *mean*.'

The wonder was that no one picked on him for standing up for me. I've never understood why some people get it in the neck and others are respected. I know it isn't anything to do with being tall, or clever. Nothing like that. It's more a kind of aura that hangs around some people. It is invisible but it still works.

Gervaise and I weren't even really friends, and didn't sit near one another. He was two desk rows forward, and to the side. But still, whenever things round me got rowdy in unsupervised prep, or when the teacher had gone from the room, he used to leave it for a little while, then lift his head and say, 'Leave Lop alone now.'

And they would.

'It's like gorillas,' Dad explained. (He bought a book about them on holiday last year and kept on reading chunks aloud. Mum got so fed up that she moved her poolside chair miles away, but I stayed to listen. That meant I knew exactly what he was trying to say because gorillas go around in groups, and some are natural leaders and others followers.)

I also think it was Gervaise who told Mrs Harper I was crying in the night. Anyway, she moved us all round. She made this giant fuss of putting Roy into a cubicle with Sam because they were best friends. That meant Liwei shared only with Shoi-Ming, but Mrs Harper said that as the two of them had to speak English all day, it was quite nice that they could take a break and chat to one another at night in Cantonese without seeming rude and cliquey.

Then, once she'd shifted a couple of the others into the dormitory for six, that left just me.

Left over. Last one picked again.

'Oh dear,' she said, as if it came as a surprise. 'I suppose that, till someone else comes, you'll have a room to yourself. Will you mind that?'

I tried to look a tiny bit disappointed. But all I really wanted was to hug Gervaise. I need a lot of time to be alone. I always have. Even way back when I came home from nursery, I used to put on headphones to blot the world out. I'd have them over my ears even before Mum slid in some music. She'd give me apple and banana slices to keep me going, and I'd sit there at least an hour.

(She said that once she lifted off the headphones before I was ready, and I tried to bite her. I don't remember that.)

Primary school wasn't too bad because they had a Friendship Bench. If you sat there, all of the bossy people in the school would come and sweep you off to play with them. So that meant if, like me, you were quite happy wandering around the playground edges, nobody bothered you. Sometimes a ball would land in front of me and I would try to kick it back. And miss. Some of the children giggled. But usually I managed to pretend I hadn't seen it till it was too late.

Secondary school was awful. I don't even want to think about how miserable I was. There was this girl who used to pick on me. Her name was Aileen Defoe and she was *horrible*. So spiteful! Forever rolling her eyes at the way I walked, mocking the way I talked, and whispering about me in corners. But she was clever about it. So when my mother came in to complain, the head made sympathetic sounds but basically she said it was 'the give and take of school' and it was up to me to harden up a bit.

That's when my parents borrowed money off my grandparents to send me here. So I don't like to let on to my family that I'm unhappy. But one day Gervaise burst into the gardener's shed and found me crying.

He watched me for a moment, then he said,

'Cheer up. You ought to know school's stupid anyhow.'

I looked up. 'What do you mean?'

'Think about it. They shove twenty of us all together in a class. The only thing we have in common is our age. Other than that, we couldn't be more different. Some are amazingly tall, like Julian. Others are tiny, like Liwei. Some are as clever as Olivia. Others are really thick.'

'Like me.'

He just ignored this. 'None of us come from the same sort of home. Half of us don't even come from the same *country*. Some love sport. Others hate it. Some of us like doing fiddly art things, while people like me get ratty every single time we have to paint, or muck about with clay—'

I interrupted him. '*And*,' I said bitterly, 'some of us like it here and others can't wait to be back home.'

He kept on. 'What's so crazy is that they herd us all into one room and say, "Right now! Get on with one another. No squabbling. Oh, yes – and did I mention that, even though every single one of you is different from the others, you'll be expected to learn things *exactly the same way*!"' Now he was grinning. 'See? It's *daft*.'

I don't know why the things he'd said had cheered me up, but I admit they had. 'I suppose it is.'

He brushed some soil off the potting-shed

shelf, and hitched himself up. 'I'll tell you what annoys me most,' he said. 'It's that they act as if it's *good* for us to be in school, when really everybody knows that we should all be taught completely differently, however suits us best.'

'They couldn't do that. They'd need millions more teachers.'

'Maybe they couldn't. But there's no reason why they have to be so smug about the way things are now. You'd be miles happier at home. So would Shoi Ming. Valentina's only here till she learns English properly. And poor Olivia *hates* it.'

'How did you get to *know* so much?' I asked him. (I had nearly said, 'How did you get to be so *kind*?' but stopped myself in time.)

'Practice,' he said. 'I'm going to be a detective when I leave school. So I watch everyone.'

'Do you keep notes?'

'Aha!' Gervaise said. 'That would be telling.'

He slid off the potting bench. 'There goes the bell.'

That's how it started. Gervaise set me thinking, and on my next weekend home I made Mum take me to a massive stationery store to buy a notebook. It was a deep forest green. One side of every double page was lined, the other plain.

'What do you want it for?' Mum asked. 'Something for school?'

'In a way.'

Then I prowled round the house to find Dad's holiday book. I finally spotted it on a shelf in the hall. It looked faded and blotchy, and when I opened it a little spill of sand fell from the spine. The author had spent years watching gorillas, charting the friendships and fights. (Gorillas get in sulks and fusses just like people do.) She wrote the whole lot down. It took me all of Saturday to read the book from start to finish. Then, on Sunday morning, I read some parts over again, even more carefully.

After our lunch on Sundays, Mum drives me back to school. 'You're ready earlier than usual.'

I looked down at my bag, already packed. 'I suppose I am.'

'Keen to get back?'

'No, not exactly.'

But I was. I started on the notebook that very night. As soon as I was by myself in my small room, I opened it to write the title page, and then the list of contents. (I did that in pencil so I could change things round if I'd missed something important out, or wanted to add other things later.)

I knew enough to get going. I already knew the people in my class who go round together all the time. I knew who was in whose gang, and who were the leaders. I knew the ones who had friends in another form. I knew the ones who like to get together and chat in their home language: the little Russian gang, the three from Singapore, the separate Chinese group.

I'd spent enough time being teased for dropping catches and fluffing kicks to know which people in our year turn into Shouters and Pushers out on the sports field. And I knew who's always first to hush the rest of the dorm each time Jean-Marc starts whispering one of his weird French ghost stories after lights out.

So I set out my groups and circles, with neat printed names. (A circle for each separate set, some of them interlocking.) I made my charts the same as all the ones in the gorilla book, except I took great care to use false names. I keep the key inside my revision maths book. No one else goes near that. And if they did they wouldn't know how the two lists were linked unless they had my forest-green notebook open in front of them as well.

I keep that even more hidden.

So now that's how I pass the time. I keep an eye on everyone around me. Most people usually hang around with the same people, but on really windy or wet days there is a lot of swapping about — I don't know why, except that maybe they get a bit over-excited. If two of the main bossies in a circle fall out, things can get very interesting, with even peaceable people taking sides and whispering in corners. When Tamara came back from having a really bad flu at home, her whole group had split up for good. Marcia and Pip had started tagging on to girls in another class, and Jodie was off with the gang who shoot goals every break time. So poor Tamara was on her own till Gervaise noticed, and told her Paul and Shoi-Ming needed one more person before Mr Appleton would start a pottery club.

And I already know from the gorilla book that, if someone new starts at our school next term, there'll be all sorts of interesting changes.

With all this watching, I am on the edge of things again, just like in primary school. But I like that. And these days, if someone makes the effort to be mean to me, I almost enjoy it. (Well, not *enjoy* it exactly. But it does make life far more interesting.) I'll notice who sets off the teasing, and who pitches in at once, like with gorillas, just to suck up to the leader. And how the ones like Poppy and Gervaise don't throw their weight about, but still have special powers. They only have to lift their heads and say, 'Lay off Old Lop. He can't help being clumsy,' and everyone backs off.

One day last week, Mrs Harper sidled up while I was sitting on the mud-room floor, still struggling with my wellies after everyone else had gone. 'Daniel, you've been in that little bedroom cubby all by yourself for quite a while now. Do you fancy moving back into the dorm?'

'No, thanks,' I said. 'I'm really happy where I am.'

And I am, too. After so many hours of being with the rest of them, I like my time alone. Some days are really busy with quarrels and fights, and people stealing other people's friends, and others storming off in sulks. It's hard to keep in mind all of the things I'll want to jot down in my notebook the moment I am on my own. I have to pay attention.

I ought to thank Gervaise for all those things he said. Because, these days, I'm really, really glad that I am usually the Last One Picked.

I put the book down thinking, good old Lop. Talk about, 'If you get given lemons, make lemonade'. I was still thinking about the story when Mum came back.

'How was Miss Shefford, then?'

'She sent her love.'

'To *me*? She doesn't even know me. We've never even *met*.'

'Sam, when you reach her age, there aren't that many people left that you can send your love to, even through someone else. So just be grateful.'

She sounded irritable, so I kept quiet. We drove for quite a while and then pulled up outside a bungalow that had four separate signs outside about not blocking the driveway.

Mum pointed all the way across the park on the other side of the road. 'See over there?'

'Those shops?'

'Yes. You could walk over and get something for

our supper. That way you'd get a breath of air while I'm with Mr Vanbrugh.'

'Those shops are *miles* away. By the time I get over there, you'll have come out again.'

'I doubt that very much.'

I glanced down at *Away From Home*. All that I wanted was to stay in the car and get on with the next story. So I tried cunning. 'I don't think that's very wise. If anyone notices me, they might ask questions.'

'Questions?'

'Yes. About what I'm doing dribbling about on a park during school hours.'

'You wouldn't be "dribbling about", Sam. You'd be walking briskly across to do some sensible shopping.'

'It might not look that way to other people.'

Mum turned sarcastic. 'You mean the same way "having a terrible stomach ache" can look like having a blue moon day?'

I changed the subject fast. 'What's Mr Vanbrugh like?'

'He's very nice and brave. Mostly I need to check he's getting on fine with all his equipment.'

'Equipment?'

'The stuff that keeps him ticking along in his own home.'

I couldn't think of anything except a walking frame. 'Like what?'

She ticked it all off on her fingers. 'His wheelchair and ramps. His walking trolley and his mobility scooter. His bath lift and bath step and grab rails. His long-handled bath washer and his non-slip bath mat. His toilet safety surround. His bed rails and adjustable back rest. His eye-drop dispenser and his seven-day pill organizer. His large-faced clock. His long-handled reacher-grips and sock puller. His neck-cord magnifying glass and big button phone. His non-slip kitchen step stool and his special jar opener. His—'

'Please stop!'

I sat there quietly while she sorted out her sheets of paper. Then, as she clipped them together, I admitted, 'Old age. It's not for wimps, is it?'

'He isn't even old,' she told me. 'He simply has a horrible degenerative disease.'

I suddenly saw why she'd been so dismissive of my stomach ache. But I still didn't want to waste time walking across the park. 'I'll tell you what,' I said. 'I promise I'll make a spaghetti supper when we get back. And as for getting a breath of air, I'll open the window.'

She gave me an affectionate swipe as she went off. I sat there for a while, and realized I was back to thinking about Daniel in the last story. I wondered what his medical problem was, to put it in the books with its own name, and make it hard for him to pull his wellies on and off.

I really hoped he didn't have a degenerative disease, like poor Mr Vanbrugh. I wondered what I would have thought about Lop if he'd been in my school. Would I have pretended not to notice when people teased him? Or would I have tried to be as kind and helpful as Gervaise? School can be hard enough, without people being mean. And if you have an extra problem, like Lop clearly did . . .

To shake off all my gloomy thoughts, I started on the next story.

Showing Round
Mr Hastings

That's the front door. Oh, I suppose you came in that way, didn't you? So you've already seen it. We're not allowed to use that door unless we're showing someone round the school, like I am you. Or maybe if we're carrying something for a teacher. Then we might be allowed to walk in with them. Otherwise we have to use the door behind the kitchens.

Unless it's raining, of course.

Why 'of course'?

Mostly because it floods along that back corridor in wet weather. That's how Stuart broke his leg. Yes, it *was* pretty bad. Mr Tanner kept saying that people our age only ever get what he called 'green stick' fractures, and that they heal so fast it's barely worth bothering to go to hospital to get an X-ray. But Matron insisted. And it turned out that Stuart's leg was really badly broken. Tom Hayter from 3B said that he saw the leg bone sticking through the skin, but no one believes that because Tom tells an awful lot of lies. He once told me he'd seen a spider crawling in my mouth while I was fast asleep, and that I swallowed it. I don't think that was true.

At least, I hope it wasn't.

How long was Stuart off school? Oh, hours! There was a massive queue at X-ray. He wasn't back till after supper, and had to go back the next day to get a proper cast. He clonked about for weeks, and Mr Tanner said it was like living in a boarding house with Long John Silver, except that he was probably a whole lot handier with crutches.

Long John Silver, that is. Not Stuart.

No, he didn't go home. No one goes home unless they're leaving for good because of crying all the time, or families running out of money. I don't suppose he would have wanted to in any case because his parents live in Dubai, and Matron said she changed planes there once, and even though the air conditioning was on full blast, it was so hot she melted. She told Stuart that wearing a leg cast in Dubai would have been murder, and he was much better off clonking around with us, and not falling behind with his maths.

The hall's through there. Do you really want to look? It's awfully boring. See? Just a plain wooden floor and walls.

What are those weird blue streaks across that wall? No, they're not art. They're my fault, actually. While we were painting the backcloth for the play a few weeks ago, I tripped and spilled a full bucket of sky-blue paint. We mopped it off the floors, but by the time we got round to wiping down the walls, the colour had sunk in.

Punished? No, I don't remember being punished. Oh, yes I do! But it was only by Mr Tanner. He got quite ratty about the sky-blue knees on his new trousers from the cleaning up, and made me write, "I mustn't be so clumsy," ten times in French.

Why French? I don't know. I never thought to ask. But I can still remember what it was: *'Je dois faire plus attention.'*

You say that's not exactly how a French person would pronounce those words. Oh, well. I needn't worry about that. I don't learn French. I just asked Mrs Lanvier to write it out for me, and then I copied it. Me, I take Cantonese.

Yes, *lots* of us do Cantonese.

Why? I don't know. I have heard Mr Tanner claim that by the time people my age reach the sixth form, there'll be so many pupils from Beijing in his maths class that he will probably have to *teach* in Cantonese. Min Joo says that's a joke, but either way those of the rest of us who opted to learn Cantonese will probably be ready.

Now, here's the dining room. All that mess on the floor will be mopped up before we come in here again for supper.

Probably.

The food? Well, actually, the food's quite good. On Friday nights we always have really nice blood and worms, and—

Sorry? No, not *real* worms. Or real blood. That's what we call spaghetti in tomato sauce. The shepherd's pie is brilliant too. And anyone who's vegetarian gets tons of those piles of grey stuff. What are they called? Hummous and couscous, is it?

Yes, I'd describe it as grey. Why? Shouldn't it be? Now, look! See that boy there! Well, he eats special buns. Not much else. Ever. None of the rest of us would be allowed to get away with that. But I think that's because his name is Celia.

No. We all call him *Hugo*. But Mr Tanner did explain that Hugo was allowed to eat some things that are different from the rest of us because he was Celia.

Coeliac? No, I don't believe I've ever heard that word.

Odd? Well, to be truthful, since you ask, I didn't think that Hugo's parents giving him a girl's name was all that odd. I did think it was strange that they let him eat special buns. But that sort of favouritism happens in this school a lot. You take Eric Wright. He doesn't have to play soccer.

Some people say that's a good thing because he would be rubbish anyway, what with his being paralysed from the waist down, and in a wheelchair. But Franklyn was in a wheelchair for weeks after he broke his femur falling off the ropes in gym, and he made a really mean goalkeeper. Everyone wanted him to be on their team.

Yes, I suppose there are a lot of broken bones. Still, 'not to worry', as Mr Tanner says.

Up these stairs are the dormitories. I'll show you mine first. See? I sleep in here. And up these stairs and round this corner is the one for girls. It's just the same except the heating works, so it's a whole lot warmer. See that bed over there. That's Martha's and it's nearest to the radiator that works best. So that's the bed that Mr Tanner gets in when he tells us ghost stories.

No, no. Martha gets out. She gets in bed with Thalia or Rhiannon.

Yes, *every* night, except when Mr Tanner has a date and has gone into town. But if he's here, he always tells us creepy stories. We like ghouls best. He does a really good ghoul wail. We've all been practising. Want to hear mine?

Yes, it is *very* ghouly, isn't it? That's what we do to make Mr Tanner come upstairs. We all make ghouly noises till the rest of the staff order him up here just to shut us up. Yes, we can all fit in – except for Simon. He has to stay alone in the boys' dorm until the story's over because he has nightmares. Terrible, terrible nightmares. He couldn't even stay in the room when we were reading some bits of *The Silver Sword* around the class.

Maybe not the best place for someone as sensitive? I don't know about that. His dad's in the army, so staying home would probably be worse. Killing and bombs and stuff. And people are very kind to him, especially the girls. They give him all the soppy old-fashioned books their great-aunts choose for them, so he'll have something not at all scary to read while Mr Tanner's with the rest of us, telling ghoul stories.

Yes, he makes all of them up. That's why his ghouls are even scarier than his ex-wife.

I don't know. How should I know? I've never been married. That's just how he describes them. He says stuff like, '*And there she stood beside the rusty graveyard gate. What little was left of her hair fell in a reeking filthy tangle, and soil from the freshly dug-up grave slid from her shroud. She turned her empty eye-sockets his way.*' And on and on. But then he always ends up with the words 'and she was even scarier than my ex-wife.' We always chant that bit along with him, just like when people say Amen along with the head, Mr Hawkins, when they're in chapel.

No, I don't go. I'm Jewish, so I clean my shoes. So do the Muslims. And the committed atheists.

What's a *committed* atheist? That's easy. That is someone who has got a note in their school file. It can't be forged, though. They're quite strict about that. They always get in touch with home to check your parents wrote it. But if they did, you get to clean your shoes instead, like all us Jews and Muslims and the like.

If they're already clean? Well, then you clean them again, unless you want to do windows. But nobody does because you have to traipse miles to the cleaning cupboard just to fetch the bucket, and miles to take it back. You would be crazy not to just sit down with everyone else, and clean your shoes again until class starts.

When do we start? Eight-fifty sharp, except for Mr Tanner, who is often late from checking on his snails.

No, not pets. They're ones he's caught on his own private veggie patch. We get to vote on how he kills them. Sometimes the vote comes out for drowning them in beer. (My dad does that as well.) And sometimes he just tosses them over the wall, saying they must take their chances.

No, we don't mind. Some of us did, especially Simon. But then Mr Tanner showed us this nature film about how song thrushes pick up snails with their beaks and bash them against rocks to get at their insides, and after that most of us reckoned Mr Tanner's snails were really lucky.

Meet Mr Tanner? Probably. Especially if I show

you round the gardens. He's often doing what the caretaker calls 'skulking behind the shed'.

Why 'skulking'? That's because he's not allowed to smoke in front of us. He shouldn't really be smoking in the grounds at all, but Mr Hawkins pretends he doesn't know because Mr Tanner is the only one who can draw up the timetable and not have everyone trying to use the hall at the same time, or have two classes being taught by the same person at both ends of the school. He's *frightfully* clever.

Yes, we all like him a lot. That's why I'm learning Cantonese, so I can carry on with maths lessons when I'm in the sixth form.

Yes, I know Min Joo said that was a joke. But I'm not sure. And you can't ever be sure with Mr Tanner. Miss Norton says he's a wild one.

Who is Miss Norton? She's the art teacher. We're making felt this term. I don't know what it's for, but it's good fun and Mr Tanner says if it's no use to anyone when it's all finished, he'll use it as an extra blanket because he's freezing at nights. He keeps on telling us that if his room gets any colder, he'll be obliged to propose to one of his girlfriends, just to have someone to cuddle to keep warm.

Yes, we know quite a lot about his girlfriends. The one he has now is called Madeleine and she has toffee-coloured hair — not the sort in the wrappers but those square loose ones that you get out of the jar. And she hates coconut ice.

Well, I thought that was knowing quite a lot.

That? Down in the courtyard? That's the school well. Someone fell down it and drowned.

No, no. That was about *a thousand years ago*. It's filled in now. That broken thing behind is what is left of the gardener's wheelbarrow. We use that for races. Len Fung fell out of it last week and scraped the whole side of his leg, and yesterday he got detention from Mr Tanner for irritating him in maths by picking at his scabs.

Yes. There are lots of detentions. Sometimes we have to write out something in French, like '*Je dois faire plus attention*'. I told you about that. Sometimes we have to clean windows. They are quite fiddly, especially those tiny lozenge-shaped ones in Main House, so Mr Bartle – he's the caretaker – quite likes it when we're ordered to do those. And Cook's in league with Mr Tanner to be extra strict with us before Fancy Dinner Night, so she can get some help cleaning the silver.

No, Fancy Dinner Night's not a treat for us. We're not invited. That is the evening when Mr Hawkins sucks up to the richest parents. Last year he only needed to scrape up enough to get the roof mended over the back corridor. But Gregory overheard Mr Tanner telling Mrs Rogers that Mr Hawkins is taking a frightful risk this year by serving only something vegetarian, hoping that

Harmanjeet's parents will cough up enough to get the swimming pool fixed.

Not that bad, no. I mean, it leaks. And it has mould. And horrid green slimy algae. But Mrs Rogers says we should be *interested* because algae is perfectly fascinating, and to make up for all our slimy swimming she will put plenty of questions about algae into this term's biology exam.

Yes, we have lots of exams, and I quite like them.

Why?

I've never thought. But now you mention it, it might be because everyone's quiet. For a whole hour and a half! Does *your* boy like exams? Or maybe it's a girl you're thinking of sending here?

You don't *have* any children? But if you've got no children, why did Mr Tanner ask me to show you round the school?

Because you're an inspector?

Of Health and Safety?

Whoops!

That cheered me up.

Shortly before I finished the last page, Mum hurried out of Mr Vanbrugh's bungalow to check I hadn't died of stomach ache.

Or been kidnapped.

(Or gone off shopping.)

'You're still all right?'

'I'm fine.'

'I shall be ten more minutes.'

'I'll still be here,' I said. 'Unless, of course, I've died of stomach ache. Or I've been kidnapped.'

I took care not to add on, 'Or gone shopping' in case Mum picked up that idea again, and walking all the way across that park to buy our supper kept me from finishing the story I was busy reading and getting on to the next.

My Perfectly Real and Not At All Invented Crisis of Faith

The problem is, I don't believe in God. I used to. Back in the nursery school I'd stand in one of our slightly wobbly 'straight lines', hands together, eyes closed. I'd chant the words that didn't mean a thing to me, but I knew off by heart.

In primary school we simply bowed our heads. By then, I'd had enough classes with Father Anselm to understand what the prayers meant. This is a very religious school, so most of us have known when to stand, when to kneel and how to behave in chapel since we were tiny.

And then, last week, while I was sitting there, I suddenly thought, 'I don't believe a word of any of this. It is all *nonsense*.'

I think that Sister Mary Eunice must have seen me staring round at the bowed heads because she sent for me straight after morning prayers. 'Cecilia? Can you explain your lack of attention this morning?'

I wasn't sure if I should come straight out with it. After all, I could have spun Sister Mary Eunice any old yarn about why I'd been distracted. Then I could just have kept going through the daily mumbo-jumbo, bowing my head at the right times, muttering anything I liked in place of the real words, thinking about whatever I liked. Why would I worry about a bit of head bobbing – especially if there was no God to look into my heart and know I wasn't taking any of it seriously.

But then I thought, to hell with that.

And so I told her. 'I've stopped believing there is any God.'

I could tell she was startled. But nuns always play it cool. Moving towards the window, she pointed to the garden and the rising moors beyond the high stone wall. 'Cecilia! Just look! The world! It's beautiful! Who else but God could have created something so special and majestic?'

I let my eyes follow her pointing finger, but I still argued. 'Oh, yes. I do see that it's hard to understand how all that fabulous stuff like flowers and clouds and sunsets and oceans got here in the first place. But there's no point in trying to explain one mystery by just inventing one that's even bigger.'

Whoops. Sister Mary Eunice's eyes were

narrowing. Perhaps she had assumed this interview would be a whole lot easier. (I am not noted in this school for instant brain power.) She breathed out slowly through her nose. (I heard her whiffling.) And then she lifted the old-fashioned watch she keeps pinned to her bosom. 'Where are you supposed to be now, Cecilia?'

'In double French,' I said.

'Right, then. You run along to that. And I'll arrange for you to have a chat with Father Anselm. He will advise you.'

I thought it would sound rude to say that I would only want to take advice from someone like Father Anselm if I believed in God. And now I didn't, his religious views meant nothing to me.

So I kept quiet and went off to double French.

Father Anselm steepled his fingers and leaned towards me over the desk. 'Cecilia, my dear, you know that I am here to *listen*. Tell me your problem.'

'No problem,' I assured him. 'I've simply stopped believing there's a God.'

He reeked of fatherly calm. 'And can you tell me why?'

'No reason in particular.'

'Surely there must be some cause for this sudden wobbling.'

'I am not *wobbling*,' I told him. 'I am quite

sure. And there are plenty of good reasons not to believe.'

He looked a tiny bit smug. 'So would you care to itemize them for me?'

He put the tiniest bit of sarcasm into 'itemize'. I reckoned he was pulling rank: *I am the trained priest. You're just the silly schoolgirl.*

That did annoy me so I let him have it.

'Well, obviously the first reason is the appalling way that the world runs. Half of it's absolutely *horrible*. Wars, plagues and famines. Refugee children. The sick. The homeless. All these unhappy people we keep raising money to help. They're around just as much as Sister Mary Eunice's lovely flowers and sunsets. If God created them he must be pretty mean, or really careless. Whichever it is, I don't feel like worshipping someone like that any longer. In fact, I think it's actually a whole lot more *polite* to just assume he isn't there.'

That mystified him. 'More *polite*?'

'Well, yes. Wouldn't you be ashamed if this was your creation? Wouldn't you think you could have done a whole lot better and fairer job if you'd tried harder?'

I noticed Father Anselm looked more tired than shocked. 'Ah-ha!' he said. 'I see you've stubbed your little toe on the age-old Problem of Evil!'

He had annoyed me again. 'Stubbed my little

136

toe!' How petty can you make somebody else's serious objection sound?

I was so cross I missed the next bit. When I tuned in again, Father Anselm was pedalling on about how very important it was that everybody had free will. 'There'd be no point in a world in which we were all well-programmed robots, going around being good and happy with no effort at all on our own parts.'

'I think that would be rather nice,' I said. 'A whole lot better. Especially for everyone who has a really rotten time through no fault of their own because of the way the world runs now.'

'Cecilia, we are not living in a day care nursery. The Lord leaves us to make our own moral choices.'

'Most of the time they're not choices,' I said stubbornly. 'Like when a thousand people die in an earthquake or a tidal wave.'

'These are great tragedies,' said Father Anselm almost as solemnly as if his pronouncement might come as news to me. 'And yet God's mercy is around us every day.'

I have been hearing this since I was three. This was the first time I had ever queried it.

'Is it? But where?'

'Where?'

'Yes. Where?'

I think I must have rattled him a bit. He blinked behind his rimless specs and spread his hands the way he does in chapel. 'Think of the miracles.'

'I would,' I said, 'if they were happening all the time, when they were needed. But they're so rare. There seem to me to be a lot more' – it wasn't a real word, but was the best I could do – 'horracles. And they are always so much bigger and nastier.'

'Cecilia, I hope I am not hearing you being flippant.'

That made me really cross. I didn't reckon it was fair to let yourself get in an argument about whether God exists, and then expect the other person to stay polite and respectful about something they're claiming isn't even there. I let Father Anselm have it. 'And that's another thing! I hate the way hundreds of people die in an earth-quake, then five days later someone pulls a crying baby out of the rubble and calls it "a miracle". I don't think that's a miracle at all! I think it's a horrible tragedy with one lucky baby.'

'Cecilia, it's not for us to presume to under-stand the ways of the Lord.'

'The trouble is,' I said, 'that people do. You do, as well. And all the Sisters. You're always telling us that God's all-knowing and all-powerful and all-loving. So either he doesn't know about the earthquake so isn't all-knowing, or he can't stop it happening and isn't all-powerful. Or else he's not all-loving.'

138

I added sourly under my breath, 'Just really *spiteful.*'

Father Anselm must have the sharpest ears. '*What* did you say, Cecilia?'

I backed off quickly. 'Nothing, Father.'

I'd gone too far. He had to press his lips together not to snap at me. But priests have loads of practice in staying calm, and in the end he tried to be conciliatory. 'I will admit that God's ways can appear to us to be deeply mysterious.'

'Not just *mysterious*,' I said. 'They're seriously weird. I mean, one minute it's an eye for an eye and a tooth for a tooth, and the next it's you must turn the other cheek and go the extra mile. One minute everyone must have free will and tragedies will happen. The next, he's sending plagues or holding back the waters of the Red Sea to help people over.'

'The inconsistencies we sometimes think we see—'

But I was in full flow. 'Helping like that shouldn't be switched on and off just when God feels like it. When Sister Bernadette wrote on my last report, "Cecilia can do well when she chooses," she didn't mean it as a *compliment*. She meant it as a *complaint*.'

He'd had enough. Steepling his fingers again, he said to me somewhat frostily, 'How long have you been with us in this school, Cecilia? Since you were four? I'd no idea that all the efforts we had

139

made to keep you close to the Lord had turned you into such a steely theologian.'

'I'm not trying to be clever,' I told him. 'I just woke up yesterday morning and wondered what the world would be like if there was no God at all. And I decided it would look exactly the same.'

'But what about *you*?' he asked me.

I hadn't got the faintest idea what he was getting at. I just sat quiet for a moment or two, and then I had to ask him, 'What *about* me?'

'If God did not exist, would you be just the same?'

He watched me thinking. In the end I said, 'Yes. Yes, I think I would. I don't think the only reason I try to be good is because God is watching. I think I truly believe that's the right way to live. So, yes, I think I'll carry on the same.'

'But doesn't God mean something to you—' He paused. 'In your *heart*? Someone who loves and cares for you. Wouldn't abandoning your God feel just like being lost – far, far away from home?'

'Away from home?'

'I mean it simply *metaphorically*, Cecilia. I mean, you know you have a special place in God's heart. He cares about you. You are safe in Him. He knows you. You know Him.'

I shook my head. 'I think I'll be all right.'

He sighed. 'All of us here do realize that faith and belief are sometimes shaken. And I am grateful that you've been so honest. I can't say that I believe you're right. In fact, I think the problem might be that you're cross with God for not being more what you want. I'm sure you wouldn't be criticizing Him so much if you didn't think He was there.'

Now he was looking rather smug again. He finished up, 'So I'm just going to ask you to go away and pray.'

'I can't pray. I've got nobody to pray to, and anyway if praying worked every children's hospital would be empty.'

'Well, try!' he said, a little sharply. 'Nothing worthwhile comes easily. And the Sisters and I will take care to pray on your behalf.'

'Thank you,' I said, but only because that seemed polite.

Next it was Mother Superior. She sent for me a few days later. She didn't exactly ask me straight out how I was doing with my spiritual life, but she did say that Sister Mary Eunice and Father Anselm had spoken to her about me. Fingering the crucifix she wears around her neck, she warned me that people my age can think too much about what she called 'complicated doctrinal matters'.

'Most of it isn't complicated at all,' I told her. 'I've just stopped believing in God. And I can't think of any reason to start up again.'

Was her look slightly mocking? 'And so, Cecilia, you feel quite confident about setting your face against millennia of belief?'

'I think I do,' I said.

Like Sister Mary Eunice and Father Anselm, she sighed. 'And there is nothing I can help you with?'

'Not really.'

She clearly wasn't going to let it go at that. 'I'm told by Father Anselm that you are particularly troubled by the problem of suffering in the world.'

'I can't see the point of it,' I admitted. (I meant to shut up after that. But she was sitting waiting.) 'I mean, maybe it's just a test, like poor Job with his painful boils and losing his family and stuff. But just like any other test, it isn't really fair. If you've a good maths brain you can bag marks a lot more easily. If you've the strength to love God even when he's being horrible' – I saw her wince at that – 'it's because he made you that way.'

While I was talking she had put on her 'I'm being patient' look. If she'd not been a Mother Superior, she would have rolled her eyes. But she should not have pulled me out of pottery in the first place if she didn't want to listen. So I kept on.

'And if suffering isn't a test at all, but more a punishment for man's old bad behaviour, like Adam and Eve eating the apple in the Garden of

Eden when they'd been told not to, then it isn't fair that babies and small children are made to suffer. They've done nothing wrong.'

In for a doctrinal penny, in for a pound. I added grumpily, 'As for the idea of Hell – I simply can't believe that any reasonable God would want anyone to go somewhere so hateful. *Ever.*'

There was the longest silence. Then she said something really nice. 'Cecilia, I am impressed with you. You've clearly thought about these matters a good deal. You've raised the questions that have worried deeply religious people all through their lives. In all the years that I've been teaching, I don't think anyone has ever stood in front of me and put their case so bravely. Indeed, you've been so bold you could be one of those saints and martyrs we so richly cherish.'

I got suspicious. 'You're not going to *exclude* me, are you?' I asked, dead worried.

'Of course not, dear! We think you very, very precious.'

I still didn't trust her. 'So what's going to happen now?'

'We shall all pray for you, of course.'

I was horrifed. 'Not the whole school!'

'Not in your own name, dear. Just for all who are struggling with doubt.'

'It isn't doubt,' I told her stubbornly. 'It's a lot more than that.'

'All right then, for all who see themselves as

undergoing a crisis of faith.' And since my ears are quite as sharp as Father Anselm's, I quite distinctly heard her irritably muttering to herself, 'Real or invented.'

I thought that was a rotten cheek. I mean, talk about two-faced! First she goes on about how much I've clearly thought about these things. She almost gives me a gold star for my grasp of 'doctrinal matters'.

And then she as good as lets it out that she thinks I'm faking to get attention, like Lucy Monteland when she 'faints' in class.

So that's how we go on. I am polite in chapel. I don't exactly bow my head, but I don't stare round any more at all the others. I will not even mouth the words, but all the Sisters take good care not to see that.

I wondered quite a lot about what Father Anselm said about my missing God's good care and feeling away from home. I don't, though. I feel fine. I don't miss praying. I don't even feel as if some giant log of belief has rolled off my shoulders.

I feel just the same.

Sometimes I look around at all the others and think, 'Could I be missing something?'

But I'm not. And then I think about that bit in my old *Alice in Wonderland* book – the bit in the second story, *Through the Looking-Glass*, when

Alice says that she sees nobody on the road and the king says, 'I wish I had such eyes. To be able to see Nobody! And at that distance too!'

My dad and I always used to share a chuckle over that (once he'd explained the joke).

The moment Mum got back in the car, she noticed how far through the book I'd read.

'You're fairly tanking through that.'

'I am enjoying it,' I told her. 'I can't think why I never read it before.'

'Was it the title put you off?'

'*Away From Home*? I don't know. Maybe it was.'

We set off, back towards the by-pass. As we were passing the massive garden centre where she lost me once when I was three, she asked me, 'Is the whole thing about boarding schools?'

'No,' I said. 'But it is mostly about people who are, or have been, sent away from home – unless, that is, the phrase is being used metaphorically.'

Good job we'd stopped at the lights because Mum almost choked. 'Did you say *metaphorically*?'

'That,' I explained, 'is when you don't mean the exact real thing, more just that something's *like* it.'

'Yes, yes. I know what it means. I was just startled that you used the word.'

'I learn a lot from things I read,' I teased. 'That's why you shouldn't ever worry when I have a stomach ache and have to stay off school.'

She let that pass and just kept driving till we reached a block of dreary-looking flats.

'Pit stop,' she told me. 'Anastasia and Wilf Huggett.'

'Great names.'

She sighed. 'I really shouldn't say this, but I swear they must be the most boring couple in the world. Obsessed with their collection of coloured-glass knick-knacks.'

She swivelled round to lift her papers off the back seat again, and she was off.

My Book About Me

I wasn't going to tell anyone at Queen Eleanor
the real truth. No way! This school is full of
people who live in houses called Manor Lodge
and The Old Rectory. Lots of them even have
ponies. Camilla's father actually owns a stud
farm. Her screen saver is a photo of a line of
horses – sorry, *hunters* – peering over their stable
doors. I'm not sure if they all belong to her father.
But he is stinking rich.

Most of the parents are.

So why would I want anyone to know my own
dead boring home address: 139 Griddell Street?
Or that my mum works in a hairdresser's. Or that
my dad (who pushed off years ago, when I was
still a baby) never worked anyway. It's bad
enough that I talk in a different way from most of
them – though I am getting better at saying
stuff the way they do: lunch, supper, hunters,
Mummy.

It was Miss Collier who sent me here. Well,

she was the one who came round to our house to nag my mum, and filled in all the forms. She said it would be wrong not to apply because the music teaching would be so much better. She said she'd never come across a girl with such a fine ear. 'If we're unlucky, then there's nothing lost. But while there are some scholarships available, it would be crazy not to have a go. A criminal waste of Angela's remarkable talent!'

She always did that – called me by my full name. Angela. And now I'm used to it. No one in this school ever shortens it to Ange. I'm only Ange again when I go home. Mum comes to fetch me on the bus. But she gets off at Cotherham, which is three miles away, and takes a taxi from there to pick me up. On our way back, she gets the driver to drop us just behind the bus station, by a large china shop. We wait in the shadow of their doorway until we see our bus pull up at the stand. Mum's never said so, but I'm pretty sure that she arranges things this way so I don't have to stand with her on the main road, along with my bags and violin and flute, while all the rest of them sail past in their posh cars.

Suppose they saw . . .

Once I'm home, everything's fine. Some friends from my old primary have dropped away, but most just tease a bit. 'Still at your posh school, Ange? Still mixing with all the snobs and toffs?'

I blush and grin, and usually they drop it. Sometimes when Teresa's at my house, she says, 'Go on, then. Show us how good you are now.' I fish out my recorder and play her something I've been practising on the flute. But then she starts to ask for things I've never heard, like songs by her favourite boy band. She tries to hum the tune, but we get nowhere and as soon as possible I put the recorder away. (I don't take out the violin or flute when I have friends around. They're only lent to me, and I'm too worried someone will damage them. My mum could never afford to get them fixed, and anyway there's no one anywhere near where we live who could repair them.)

So when Mr Wilson said that in the last two weeks of term he wanted us to write a long piece called *My Book About Me,* I felt my stomach turn. I could imagine Camilla's – all about grooming hunters. Or Bryony's – about her family's marvellous picnics down by the lake that turns out to belong to them, and is just perfect for swimming 'if you don't mind reeds'.

Then Oscar Dando asked Mr Wilson, 'Do we have to tell the truth?' (His dad's a pop star, so he's had to learn not to say anything about his family.)

'Write whatever you want,' said Mr Wilson. 'Just try to remember that it's "Life Writing" we've been talking about this term. All I want to see is a good piece of work.'

That's when I thought about the book *My Family*.

Mum found it in a charity shop when I was small. The cover showed a brother and sister on a seesaw in a cottage garden. (The girl was up, the boy down.) And it was only after Mum had read it to me that we realized it was a school book. We thought that there was still another chapter to go, but when we got close to the end we saw the last few pages were just long lists of words that had been in the stories. Next to each English word was the same word in Spanish. (Mum knew because she'd had four holidays in Spain before she had me and Dad left.)

I didn't care. I didn't think of all those Spanish children sitting in school, trying to understand the story and flipping to the back over and over to see what the English words meant: cottage, chimney, brother, cousin, holiday.

I just *adored* the stories. Everyone in them was so kind and happy. The children helped in the kitchen and played in the countryside. The family went on a seaside holiday. An aunt and uncle came to visit. The neighbour's dog got lost and the boy found it. The girl had a birthday. On Christmas Day the children made a snowman. Something nice happened in every chapter except one (the day the car broke down) and even that day ended happily.

Mum says I chose *My Family* over and over for

the bedtime read. I know I envied the girl – she was called Susan Blackett – for having a garden big enough to play in properly. And back then I was sure that nothing in the world could be more fun than having a brother like Peter. I adored Mr Blackett too. He smoked a pipe and spent a lot of time fixing things that were loose or broken. The mother was always at home to take care of the children. ('Come down that tree, Peter! You are much too high.' 'Susan, be careful! Please don't ride so fast. You might fall off your bike!')

And she was bravely learning to drive the family car.

So if I had to write about somebody's life, why not borrow the Blacketts? No one would know. I wasn't *ever* going to risk inviting one of my Queen Eleanor friends back to my own real home. I could imagine the look on even sweet Camilla's face as her mum's gleaming car pulled up outside our house.

Neither of them would realize that Mr Tenby next door has been so busy caring for his bed-ridden mother that he's no time to scrape the peeling paint off his window frames or touch up his scruffy front door. They'd see the students across the street sprawled on that ratty sofa they've never bothered to take to the dump or drag back in the house. But they would never guess that on the day Mum let the back door slam behind her in the wind and locked herself out, all four of them rushed to find someone who could lend a ladder, and they got Mum back in our house before the potatoes she'd left on the boil even went dry.

No. Far, far better to write about the Blacketts. The father's pipe would have to go, of course. No one still smokes a pipe. And if I claimed I had a brother, people would ask me why he didn't come to the same school as me. So Peter ought to be a cousin.

But most of the other things would be all right.

So I began. We have an hour and a quarter to work between tea and supper. They call it 'supervised prep', but it's just homework, like in my old school, except that you're not doing it at your own kitchen table. I wrote *My Book About Me* at the top, like Mr Wilson said, and then I stared at it. Susan in *My Family* had blonde hair and blue eyes, so I would have to change that. My hair and eyes are brown. And I thought that it would be strange to talk about 'my cousin Peter' straight away. People would think I had a crush on him. So I skipped all the bits that had him in, and started off using the chapter that was about Mrs Blackett's first driving lesson.

But it was so *dull*. I hadn't realized till I tried to write the story out as if it was my own mum, but all Mrs Blackett did in *My Family* was say hello to the instructor, get in the car and drive about a bit ('along the road, up the hill, over the bridge and round the corner'), and then get out and pay him, and say thank you and goodbye.

So I gave her a car crash. Oh, not a horrid one, with dead and injured sprawled about the place, and sirens blaring. Just a little crash, like the one Mum and I watched from the window when two of the drivers who use Griddell Street as a rat-run scraped one another's cars and stood there bellowing about whose stupid fault it was, and whose insurance company would have to pay.

There was some time left, so I did another paragraph. This time I had the chapter about Susan Blackett's birthday in mind. It started well enough, with Susan feeling happy and tearing wrapping paper off the gift her parents gave her. But in the book *My Family*, her birthday present was a doll.

Just a plain doll.

That wouldn't do. I was too old, and it was far too boring. Instead, I still pretended it was me, but wrote about the time Teresa's stepmum put the wrong date on all her party invitations by mistake. When no one came, Teresa cried so much that she threw up. And while her stepmum tried to comfort her for having such rotten friends, Teresa's dad and brothers scoffed all the sausage rolls and chocolate biscuits and cake.

That meant that when we all showed up on

time next day, there wasn't anything for us to eat.

The bell rang then. I had to go for supper. And the next night I had a pile of other things to do in prep. But the day after that, I had the time to write a bit more of *My Book About Me*.

I thought I'd better say a bit about my dad. I couldn't use my real one, obviously. I don't remember anything about him. But in *My Family*, Mr Blackett was always kind and smiling. Still, I'd had to take his pipe off him, and I remember very well what happened when Mrs Percy on our street gave up cigarettes. For six whole weeks we saw her prowling round her garden at all hours of the day and night, hunched over, muttering. Her husband Tom complained to Mum that his nice wife had turned into a ratbag fiend, and he was tempted to run away and stay with his brother in Scarborough until her craving for fags had stopped.

That sounded more realistic, so I wrote that. Then, to be fair, I did try to explain that Mr Percy wasn't perfect either. I told about the time he got drunk at the works party, caught the wrong bus, then fell asleep and ended up in Grimsby.

And then I wrote about the evening he was left babysitting, but couldn't find their baby granddaughter's nappies, so wrapped her bum up in his wife's best nightie.

And the time he came to our house with a bunch of kohlrabi Mr Singh had dropped in his vegetable order by mistake. 'What the hell is this stuff? And what am I supposed to do with it? Would it be rude to take it back?'

I was about to start in on the time he chained himself to the bandstand. (He'd just found out the council wanted to demolish it because of what he called 'a tiny patch of rot that could be sorted in half a morning'.) There was a giant punch-up at the end of that. But then the bell rang for the end of prep, so I had to cut that story shorter than I would have liked, because it ended rather excitingly in real life, with Mr Percy being led away and ticked off by the police.

By then we only had one day to finish our Life Writing. And so, to fit in everything that I liked best in the *My Family* book, I thought I'd shove a couple of chapters together and have the visit from the uncle and aunt at the same time as Christmas. (That meant that I could bring in Peter. He could be their son – my cousin – and I could add the bit about building the snowman, and hanging up the Christmas stockings.)

But there was nothing to the story when I started writing it – just all the grown-ups saying things like, 'Oh, what a pretty bedroom', and, 'Such a lovely view', and 'Here is the bathroom.'

Everyone was so *polite*.

I thought I ought to jazz it up a bit. So I put in what happened in Teresa's house when her dad's brother and his girlfriend Julie stayed for three whole weeks because they'd nowhere else to go till their new flat was ready. Julie just lolled about in bed till lunch time every day. (I would have written 'dinner time', but I was worried Mr Wilson might assume that I meant evening.) Since they were sleeping on a mattress in the living room, that drove Teresa's stepmum wild. Things kicked off with a bit of quiet niggling about the need for Julie and Steve to 'try to keep things a little tidier', and ended with great steaming rows about sodden towels and grubby clothes strewn everywhere, and make-up bottles leaking greasy stains into the carpets.

Teresa's dad was daft enough to stick up for his brother. And then real fireworks started. I can remember pretty well all of it because Teresa and I did the whole argument as a Christmas Show to cheer my mother up while she was in bed with flu. I played Teresa's dad, and Teresa did a brilliant job of being her stepmother. Mum said that our performance was every bit as riveting as all the family rows she hears about while she is trimming people's hair.

So I shoved the whole quarrel in (except for where I changed the words because I thought that Mr Wilson might not like to see great clumps of asterisks).

It went like this:

'How *dare* you? How *dare* you take the side of that messy little madam?'

'I'm not taking her side! I'm only saying it's hard to keep a room looking nice when you're having to sleep in it.'

'Only if you're so idle you sleep till noon!'

'That's not fair!'

'Don't tell *me* what's fair! It's not fair that we have to shop and cook and clean and try to work our way round that lazy pair for weeks on end!'

'It isn't "weeks on end". It's just three weeks.'

'Yes! First week! Second week! And still a week to go! I call that "weeks on end".'

'Keep your hair on! Don't forget Steve's my *brother*!'

'Don't forget I'm your *wife*!'

'A pretty bad-tempered one, too!'

'Oooh!' (Here, in our play, Teresa snatched up the frying pan, and Mum held her breath.) 'Ooooh! I could . . . I could . . .'

Still doing my part as Teresa's dad, I tried to calm her. 'Now, now, Fran! Don't go berserk! I didn't mean to say that! It slipped out!'

'Just like this pan is going to slip out of my hand – onto your stupid fat head!'

And there was plenty more where that came from. It's just that I ran out of time. The bell had gone and we were being shunted along to supper. I didn't even have time to write about making the snowman or hanging up the Christmas stockings. (It's just as well, perhaps. One snowman looks much like the next, and I couldn't even give him Mr Blackett's pipe to make him special since those days are so long gone.)

So I just wrapped up *My Book About Me* up by writing a couple of sentences about what I want to do when I'm older (be a musician – surprise!) and left it on the pile on Mr Wilson's desk.

It was a week before he gave them back. 'Here we are, Camilla. I never thought I'd ever learn so much about horses – sorry, *hunters*.' 'There you go, Bryony. I must say that your lake sounds *wonderful*.' 'Very good, Oscar. I've learned a lot about pop music but nothing whatsoever about your dad. So full marks for discretion!'

Then he came to me.

'Here you are, Toots!' (He never calls me Angela.) 'I must say yours was gripping from first page to last. Car crashes, punch-ups in the street and flaming family rows. I hope you really live such an exciting life. I'd hate to think that you're just teasing me, and if I checked I'd find that you go home to some pretty cottage with a seesaw in the front garden, and play in the country and go on trips to the seaside and make snowmen at Christmas.'

And he gave me a giant wink.

The idea of inventing a false life interested me. When Mum came back from seeing Anastasia and Wilf Huggett (and their new knick-knacks), I asked her, 'Do you think lots of people who are away at school pretend to be not who they are?'

'Not who they are?'

'I mean, make out they come from richer homes than they do, or have more interesting families and friends.'

Mum gave the matter some thought as we drove off towards her next appointment. 'I bet some of them do get rather good at hiding things because they wouldn't have to keep the deception up all the time, the way they would if friends lived close, like yours do. They could relax during each holiday.'

'I'd never get away with bigging myself up. Not with Louis next door.'

'No. He would certainly split on you.' Mum peeled off the main road, into a housing estate where everyone was clearly competing to have the fanciest garden. She pulled up outside another bungalow with bow windows, but this time, instead of reaching straight behind her for her paperwork, she sat there thinking.

Finally she confessed. 'I think what worries me is what someone away from home might be hiding. Not something trivial – like whether their mother wears weird clothes, or their father's in a wheel-chair. But something far more important – their real emotions.'

'But they would only be doing it for the weeks they're away. When they came home, they would be able to relax and let their feelings out.'

'I'm not sure it's that easy . . .'

She fell quiet. Turning to look, I realized she was staring at the broken Satnav.

Was she thinking about Dad?

She gave herself a little shake, and carried on. 'It's easy to get so much in the habit of pretending, even to yourself, that you don't feel what you feel that you lose sight of your real self. When you're with others all the time, and they are watching, it might seem simpler not to even realize that, deep inside, you want to weep, or lose your temper, or just be on your own a while.'

I thought I might as well confess. 'Having a quiet blue moon day.'

'Having a quiet blue moon day. Yes. That's what worries me. That someone might get *stuck*.'

'Stuck? You mean, keeping a stiff upper lip, and all of that?'

A strange look crossed my mother's face. 'Yes. Someone might get so into the habit of pretending that they're not having feelings that they might cross a line.'

And now I *knew* that she was thinking about Dad.

'And after that,' she added, 'it might turn out to be impossible to get real feelings back.'

She blinked as if she might have been quite close to tears. Then she swung round to snatch her paperwork off the back seat, and almost fled from the car.

I watched her hurrying up the path towards the bungalow. I knew exactly what was in her mind. Dad has to keep his feelings totally in check when he's away. He is a soldier and that is his job. He comes home with the dark look on his face, and starts to pick his daft quarrels: 'Why have you moved the garden tools?' 'How come we're always out of shoe polish when I come home?' 'Don't tell me that this fan's still broken! Can't you get *anything* done while I'm away?'

Mum puts up with it for a couple of days, rolling her eyes at me, taking deep breaths and walking out

162

of rooms. Then she lets rip. 'Don't you *dare* stroll back after so long away from home and boss me and Sam about. We're not your squaddies, to be criticized for every last stupid thing! And don't forget that we can manage very well indeed without you!'

Then there's a blazing row. They go upstairs, but I can hear their voices easily enough. Mum's usually in tears. I've even heard Dad crying once or twice. They stay up there for quite a while. But always, when they come back down, the worst is over. Over the next few days they have a lot of private talks in quiet voices, well away from me. My guess is Dad is telling Mum the things that neither one of them would ever want me to hear.

And I know quite enough about what soldiers sometimes do to make sure I don't listen.

Then things get better, day by day. Dad's dark look vanishes and he's himself again, making our favourite pancakes, patting Mum on the bum, saying nice things about how wonderful it is to be back home, moaning about the army, stealing Mum's bubble bath, falling asleep in front of the telly, having a laugh with me.

Maybe, each time my dad comes back, Mum thinks it's touch and go whether the easy-going, cheerful man who strode out of our house with all his gear can turn back into himself. Maybe she worries that, this time, he might have crossed the line and we have lost for good the man who has real human feelings.

I bet that was the reason why she never wanted me to go away to school – so that she never, ever had to cope with both of us when we came back. That's why she claimed I wasn't the type – in case I went, and then I crossed that strange, invisible line, and after that it was impossible for me to get my own real feelings back.

Yes, I bet that was what it was.

I reached out to touch the Satnav. Now I even thought I knew why Mum had never given that to Sandra next door. Sandra's an engineer. If she can't fix things, then they can't be fixed. You might as well throw them away. I reckoned Mum was leaving it broken and useless in the car for a good reason. Maybe Dad's right, and she's a brilliant strategist. Maybe she likes to keep things so she knows exactly where and when the sniping's going to start, the first aggressive shot that will be fired before the battle that they have upstairs to bring Dad back to himself.

I didn't want to think about my parents any more, so I picked up the book.

The Ladder of Fear

You'll think I'm just a wimp, but I have always had a problem going to school. Mum says that even back in nursery I'd cry unless she stayed. Everyone else's dad or mum hung about only till all the outdoor toys had been pulled from the shed. They'd pick their way between the trikes and scooters and ladybirds on wheels to kiss their child goodbye, and half the toddlers didn't even notice. A few might have been tearful and unsure for a few days. But everyone settled in quickly.

Except for me. Mum says that I was clingy, and once tugged her skirt so hard when she was trying to leave that it came off. In front of everyone!

I wasn't too bad most of the way up primary school. I had two good friends. Pash and his mum came to collect me each morning. (Her office was beside the school.) We'd run ahead, and I don't think I even noticed when we reached the gates.

Pash would charge through them on the search for Tom, and I'd just follow.

Then Pash went back to India with his family, and sometimes I missed school. I'd get up feeling fine, but then these butterflies would start in my stomach. I couldn't eat my breakfast. I kept rushing to the loo. Sometimes I'd even be shaking.

Mum would get worried. 'Josh, aren't you feeling well?'

'Not really. My stomach hurts.'

She'd lay a hand on my forehead. 'You're not feverish.'

'I'm feeling trembly, though. Especially my legs.'

Mum would look worried. But she works from home, sitting at Dad's old desk under the stairs, making phone calls about insurance. If I watch telly or play quietly on the computer, it doesn't stop her earning money. So she'd say, 'See if you feel better in a little while.'

And when I didn't, she would usually let me stay home.

So it was Mrs Bridge who realized I was missing Wednesdays – almost every week. She asked Mum in for a chat. I had to wait outside the door, then I was called in as well.

'So what's on Wednesdays, Josh?' asked Mrs Bridge. She twisted the computer round to show me the pattern, and it was true that all my absences fell on the same day each week.

I didn't answer, so she said it for me. 'Is it outdoor games?'

I hadn't realized. Honestly. I mean, I knew that when Mum said I could stay home, I'd think, 'Good. That means I'll miss Mr Kuperschmidt.' But I'd not guessed that going out to games was what had made me feel shaky in the first place.

So I was better after that. And so was he. I think that Mrs Bridge probably spoke to him. He didn't shout so much – well, not at me – and he would usually say something friendly when we ran out on the field. 'You're looking fit today, Josh.' Or, when we finished, 'Well played! Excellent footwork between you and Tom.'

Then we went up to the big school. But Tom didn't come. His dad's a Catholic, so he was sent to Cardinal Newman High. Mum said I couldn't go there too, partly because we're not Catholic, and partly because you really need a car to get to it, and since Dad left we haven't had that sort of money.

I had to go to Ashley Park.

I thought I would at least be with some other people from my primary school. But it turned out that most of those who live on the west side of the by-pass chose somewhere else. One or two just went off to other schools, or moved away. So I was on my own except for Stuart, who I didn't really know at all, and stuck-up Mandy

Brock who luckily was in a different home class.

I hated Ashley Park. It was so huge. The corridors were awful – dark, crowded and noisy. I had to elbow my way between shouting people just to get to my next class – if I could even work out where that was. I'm quite small so I kept on getting bashed by massive book bags.

I didn't like the lessons. Nobody knew your name unless you made trouble, which I don't. I kept my head down, longing for each day to end so I could get back home. The teachers never seemed to have the time to explain things at the end of class, like they did back in primary. Sometimes I wouldn't have the least idea of what I was supposed to do, or when I was supposed to hand work in. I didn't want to put my hand up so I'd think, 'I'll ask her when the buzzer goes.' But then she'd hurry out to beat the rush and I'd not see her again the whole day, not even walking down a corridor. I suppose I could have asked Stuart, who was usually in the same classes. But he was busy with his new friend Matt, and I felt stupid.

That's when I started feeling sick on more and more mornings. I wasn't faking and I wasn't bunking off. Bunkers don't let their parents know they're skipping school. They sit through registration with fat grins till they've been marked as present. After that they're off.

That wasn't how it worked with me. I didn't

want not to be there. It's just that, when it came to it, I couldn't go. I'd do my homework. (I get good marks when I know what I'm doing.) And I'd be fine all weekend – right through till Sunday night when Mum would start to nag about me packing my book bag. Then I'd feel queasy. I'd get to sleep all right. But I'd wake in the night with the most awful thoughts, feeling that something terrible was going to happen. I might imagine Mum finding out that she had cancer, or getting hit by a car, or dying in her sleep. I'd lie there feeling as bad as if it had happened. I'd even imagine her funeral, reckoning I'd be the only person there apart from Aunt Marjorie, because Dad wouldn't bother. I had whole conversations in my head with the police and funeral people. I'd cry so much I'd have to turn my pillow over or get so worked up that I'd have to sneak along to check that Mum was still alive.

Sometimes it seemed a hundred years till morning. But breakfast was worse. My stomach pains were *awful*. I'd shake and sweat. Sometimes I even threw up. My heart would go thumpety-thump as if it was bursting, and if Mum tried to force me upstairs to get in my uniform, I'd lose my temper or burst into tears.

Even if I got that far, I couldn't get myself out of the door. Sometimes Mum almost *dragged* me out and down the path. We'd set off for the school, but I'd be hanging back, pleading that I felt sick. And by the time we reached the crossing it was so late, and I was in such a state, she usually gave up.

'What are you *worrying* about?' she'd ask time and again, as if the horrid thoughts that haunted me were just plain silly.

I *hated* that. Mum worries about everything. When Dad was home late all those times, she always fretted in case he'd had a car crash. When he went off with Valerie, she was convinced we couldn't keep the house. She got the phoning job straight off, although she loathes it. But she still worries that her boss will ring her up and say that they don't need her any more.

I had at least as many reasons as Mum to worry. By then I'd missed so many days in school that I knew people must be noticing. I thought if I was forced to answer a question in class, some joker would call out, 'Who said that? None of us knows that voice!', and everyone would snigger. I had a dream that Mrs Fuller gathered up all the print-outs of the absence messages my mum had sent, and threw them in the air, and everyone laughed. I fretted that I'd make stupid mistakes because of things I'd missed. I knew that, even if I did go back, I'd probably be terrible at every-thing – especially sport. I worried that, if I stayed off, I'd fall even further behind. And then I worried that, if I did go, people would bully me.

The only time I could stop worrying was after

Mum gave up. She'd see me running to the lavatory for the tenth time and say, 'Oh, all right! You can stay home. But you must promise me you'll try to go tomorrow.'

'I promise.'

And I did mean it. But you can get quite good at putting tomorrow out of your mind. For hours I'd feel fine. The stomach ache would go. My thumping heart would settle. I'd stop feeling sick. My hands would steady enough for me to play 'Planet Attack'. And I'd be perfectly content until the evening, when she'd start up again. 'I did mean what I said. You really are going tomorrow. Do you understand?'

I'd nod. I'd feel my stomach clench, and all the feeling fine would drain away.

And then the phone call came from school. Mum was called in. This time they wanted me to be there too, right from the start. The head teacher, Mrs Palgrave, gave me the longest look over her steepled fingers. 'Two terms you've been with us now, Josh,' she said, pleasantly enough. 'But in that time you've slid from coming nearly nine days out of ten to only three and a half.'

My mother looked quite shocked. 'I'm sure that Josh comes more than that,' she tried to defend us both.

But Mrs Palgrave showed her a print-out of my attendance record. There was no pattern, like when I was skipping Wednesdays in my primary school.

There were just loads of absences.

We were in Mrs Palgrave's office quite a while. 'Josh can't go on like this. He needs an education, and he needs to be with people his own age.' She said that even though the holidays were starting, she'd be sending someone round to talk to us about the problem. She said that I was bright enough, but couldn't keep up with the work with so many days away. We had to have a plan.

I think she was expecting Mum to argue. But I could tell that Mum was pleased. She'd got herself into a state of not knowing what to do, and now it looked as if there might be a way out. At the end Mum said thank you over and over, till Mrs Palgrave said, 'You mustn't *worry*, Mrs Aranda. We'll sort this out and have Josh back in school.'

'As soon as he's better,' Mum agreed.

'No.' Mrs Palgrave put Mum right. 'Having Josh back in school again will *be* the getting better.'

She sounded quite firm about that.

And so did Tara Beckenridge when she came round. She talked to Mum first, but I listened at the door. She was as definite as Mrs Palgrave. 'All of these stomach aches and dizzy spells are just *anxiety*. Everyone gets that. It's perfectly normal, and often useful because it stops you doing stupid things without thinking. It's just that Josh's worries have got out of hand. He's like a smoke alarm that's set wrong, and goes off at the slightest whiff of a bonfire a mile away.'

I didn't get to hear much more because the kettle boiled, and Mum was clattering. But then I was called in. Tara sent Mum away, and made me sit beside her. She drew a body shape and handed me a red felt pen. 'Where does it feel the *worst*?'

I had no problem with that. I drew a circle where my stomach is.

'Where else?'

I drew a trembly shiver down the legs. I put small stabby dots all over where the heart would be to show it thumping, and jagged lines that stuck out from my brain to show me having awful thoughts. I even ran a thin line round the top half of the body shape, to show me sweating.

'Not at all nice,' she said. 'Small wonder you'd prefer to stay at home. These are bad jitters.'

She asked a heap of questions as she drank her tea. She asked if I was bullied, and sounded really pleased when I said no. She asked about my friends, and I explained that Tom and Pash had both gone somewhere else. She asked about our family, and I explained how Dad went off with Valerie, saying it really quietly in case my mum was doing the same as I had, and listening behind the door.

And then she tore a new page from her pad and drew a ladder with about twenty rungs.

'This is your Ladder of Fear,' she told me, grinning her head off as if what she was saying was a giant joke. 'Your homework. You're to do it properly. Write down the twenty worst things about going to school, and put them in order. Top of the ladder is what you worry about most. Your biggest and worst fear. Towards the bottom go things that aren't so bad. But everything must be in the right order on the rungs.'

'If it gets messy, can I start again?'

'Of course. But you must have it done by Tuesday, when I'm coming again.'

I quite enjoyed the homework. I used scrap paper to write down the worst things. Fretting that there'd be homework that I hadn't known about. Going through the black double doors. Being nagged to eat breakfast. Putting on uniform. Worrying that teachers would get mad at me. Waking up realizing it's a school day. Telling Mrs Fuller why I wasn't there the day before. Packing my school bag. Not knowing if I'm supposed to bring money for something. Changing for footie. When I get going, it's like a tap turns on inside my head. The worry spills out onto *everything*.

I hadn't realized that there were so many things that made me feel so awful. Far more than twenty! I picked the worst, and even then it took a lot of time to put them in order. Sometimes I'd think, 'That's not so bad as that.' I'd feel my stomach clench and change my mind. 'Oh yes, it is. It's *worse*.'

I did it, though. I got the ladder done. I even drew it really well, with proper shading, writing the words as neatly as I could so that they fitted in the rungs.

1. Going into the classroom and seeing every-one look round.

2. Walking through the school gates past all the people I don't know who are talking and laughing, or kicking a ball about.

On and on down the rungs. I was so proud of it that I was really glad when Tara Breckenridge phoned up to ask if she could come a day early.

She loved my Ladder of Fear. 'If this was real school homework, I'd give you an A!' She took a good long look at what I'd written, then she said, 'The trouble is, your brain's not doing you any favours at all.'

'Isn't it?'

'No. Nothing it's doing is helping. It should be trying to show you how to *solve* the problem.'

'I suppose it should.'

'Instead, your brain is giving you absolute rubbish advice. Sometimes it's simply telling you to put the problem out of your mind as long as you can.'

'Like at weekends? And now, when we're on holiday anyhow?'

'Even in term time, after your mother gives up and lets you stay home. You told me that you don't start worrying again until the evening.' She sighed. 'And sometimes your brain is even being daft enough to let you just hope for the best.'

'Thinking I might feel better tomorrow?'

'Exactly! And all the rest of the time it's simply leaving you to worry yourself sick.'

'It certainly is,' I said, because the Ladder of Fear had set me thinking quite a lot. I hadn't realized how much of my life was getting chewed up by this business of not going to school. I was a mess from fretting. I do hardly anything else. (I don't have time!) I don't go out. I can't make any friends because I'm hardly ever out of the house. I just watch films and stuff, or play 'Planet Attack' till I feel rubbish again.

But I had never thought to blame my *brain*.

Suddenly I wanted more than anything to be like other people who drift off to school each day, shrug if things go wrong, sleep at nights and get their work done without *worrying*.

'So can we fix things?'

'Of course! That's why I'm here.'

She was so sure. I was suspicious. 'How?'

'Ah, that's where Stan Smith comes in.'

* ★ ★ ★

I loved Stan from the start. He told a stupid joke
about a frog, and then sent Mum away. 'Have
coffee on the corner. I'll ring you when we're
done.'

The hour went so fast. He showed me how to
loosen my body when it got tense. 'Scrunch up
your face then let it go. Now your hands. Now
drop your shoulders. That's right. Turn your head
gently to the right. Now to the left. Gently! Don't
unscrew your head. It might fall off.'

That sort of thing.

We did deep breathing. 'Breathing *relaxes*
you. I'll count to four while you breathe in, and
then again while you breathe out. Ready?'

I was no good at it at first. But soon I
managed to slow down and he was pleased
with me.

He took a long look at my Ladder of Fear and
tapped one of the rungs. 'See this? Rung number
five. "Waking up remembering it's a school day."
What's going on in your mind?'

I tried to tell him. 'I just think that I can't do it.
I can't go.'

'Because?'

'I just can't face it. I keep thinking something
terrible will happen.'

'But nothing terrible has ever happened yet?'

In the end, I had to admit it. 'Not yet. No.'

'And chances are it never will.'

'Perhaps.'

'No. Almost *definitely*. After all, pretty well everyone else manages.'

'It's different for them.'

'That's right. It's *different*. They don't have unhelpful brains feeding them scary thoughts all day and night. That's what we're going to stop. We're going to retrain your brain to be more sensible and stop upsetting you.'

'Retrain my brain?'

'Yes! And we're going to start now.'

And so we did. I told him just a little more about the scary thoughts, and he began to teach me how to deal with them.

'You're going to learn to challenge your own brain. Put it right. After all, you're the boss. You're going to learn to tell your brain: "You stop that sort of thinking right now! You're simply *panicking*. You're being daft, and I'm not going to listen."'

He made me practise. Honestly. He made me think of all the scary thoughts I get, and told me what I had to say to my brain. It was all mostly the same, of course, over and over – telling my brain that it had got itself into a state, hair-triggered like a car alarm that doesn't wait for a smashed window but kicks off even if someone's just walking past.

He gave me homework. I was to do the breathing and relaxation exercises he had taught me every day. And talk to my brain.

'Do it out loud,' he said. 'Stand tall in front of a mirror and tick off that brain of yours until it realizes it must reset itself more sensibly, so you can go to school.'

He phoned Mum and they fixed a day for my next visit. Then he told us one last joke about a library cat. Mum had brought me a cake, and we walked home. But suddenly, as we were going under the old railway bridge, I felt this sudden surge of energy and jumped to try to touch the slimy roof, yelling for echoes, just like I used to when I was little. It was a surge of – oh, I don't know! – it felt like *happiness*. Stan was as confident as Tara Breckenridge. And I felt really hopeful too.

Yes, I was *happy*.

I had more sessions over the holidays. And on the day before the new term began, Tara Breckenridge came. 'So how's it going with Stan?'

'Good,' I said. 'He's really nice. And funny, too.'

'Doing your homework?'

'Trying.'

'I'm glad,' she said, 'because today we're going to draw up your Back to School Plan.'

'*Today?*'

'Why not? You said yourself that one of your big worries was falling further behind.'

'I know, but—'

Then I gave up, because she'd gone off to fetch Mum.

She stayed an hour. First she gave Mum a list of rules to do with me. I had to try to go to school every single day. Every single day! No excuses. Mum wasn't to listen to anything I said about stomach aches, or feeling sick or dizzy. ('He's not sick. They're only *jitters*.') She was to make me get into my uniform and take me as far as the school. 'It doesn't matter if he gets there late. He must still go. The teachers know there might be problems, but they'll be expecting him. No one will shout or tell him off. But he must go.'

'What if it doesn't work?' Mum asked. 'What if he's throwing up, or trembling so badly he can't walk.'

'He can't throw up all day. The minute he stops, you have to take him.'

'Even if half the day's gone?'

'Even if school's nearly finished. If Josh has time to get through those school gates before the last bell rings, he has to go.'

She turned to me. 'And that will be a whole lot easier than you think because of the skills Stan's taught you. The first time you get into uniform, you will feel nervous. But then you'll make yourself relax and breathe more calmly. You'll remind your brain that you're right and it's wrong. There isn't anything to fear.'

I would have loved to believe her, but I didn't. What I did was snap at her. 'That's fine for you to say! You're not me! It won't be that easy!'

She didn't seem to mind me being rude at all. 'No, it's not easy. But it's *possible*, and you can do it. The second morning, things will go faster and better. You'll not be quite so anxious as the day before. The time after that — better still! Because, day by day you'll be retraining your body and brain together. Your body will get more relaxed and your brain more sensible. And since each will be helping the other out, it'll get faster and easier.'

She turned to Mum. 'Like being on a diet. Saying no to crisps and cakes is horribly difficult at first, but if you persist, it gets almost automatic.'

And I remembered Dad. He used to smoke. Sometimes at night he'd even get the car out, and drive off to buy another pack of cigarettes to see him through till morning.

Then he gave up. It took him a few goes, and he was really ratty. But he did manage in the end, and then at Christmas Aunt Marjorie offered him a cigarette and he waved her pack away as if he'd never had one in his life.

I didn't want to mention Dad in case it upset Mum. So I stayed quiet.

In any case, Tara was off again. 'Just one more

thing. No screens or games at home in school hours. Not even plain old telly.' She wagged her finger at Mum. 'You're to make sure of that. Check on him! If Josh tries arguing, lock the whole lot away. He mustn't spend a single moment of the time that he's supposed to be trying to get to school on anything else but that. *Trying.* So no distractions. None.'

I must have looked appalled. Even Mum looked unsure.

'This is *important*,' Tara said. 'This is not being cruel. It's like injections – no fun while they last, but *worth* it.'

Her firmness must have rubbed off on Mum because the only thing she said to Tara was, 'When do we start?'

'Tomorrow.'

I felt my stomach lurch. But Tara handed me a little red card. 'This is from Mrs Palgrave. Keep it safe. It's your Get Out Of Class card.'

That sounded better. 'Can I use it any time?'

'No,' Tara said. 'Three times a day for the first week. The next week, twice a day at most. And after that, only the once, and only in emergencies.'

I turned it over. My name was printed on the front, and on the back there was a grid of tiny squares. 'How does it work?'

'You show it to the teacher. They tick a box, and you're allowed to slip away somewhere quiet for fifteen minutes to do your relaxation, and tell your brain to calm down.'

Now I was getting irritable again. 'You make it sound as if it *can't go wrong!*'

Would you believe it, she just smiled.

So here we are. I have to tell you the first day was *horrible.* I sweated all the time and used my card four times because one of the teachers didn't know he was supposed to mark it. I ran to the lavatories and locked myself in a cubicle. There I sat, shaking, for almost the whole fifteen minutes. But then I worried that they'd come to look for me, and that would be worse. So I did my deep breathing, and dropped my shoulders and made my fingers loose. And then I told my brain, 'Just knock it off. We were all right in there until you started up. So shut your stupid face!'

And I went back.

Next day was better. It began with lots of throwing up. But Mum insisted we still go, and watched my back till I went into school. (She probably stood there half the day as well, checking I didn't slip out.)

I got a grip and went along the corridor to find my English class, then stood outside, trying to get it together to go through the door. But Mrs Banks caught sight of me through the square of glass, and came out to fetch me, so I had no choice.

'You sit by Stuart. He'll show you what we're doing.'

I unpacked my bag, and Stuart pushed what he was writing along the double desk so I could copy it. 'Are you all right? You look dead pale.'

'I'm OK.'

Then Matt leaned back from his desk in front of us to whisper, 'Mrs Fuller said you'd not been well.'

'No,' I said, then added something Stan taught me to tell my brain. 'But I am getting better every day.'

I really am. Each morning's easier. I haven't thrown up in two weeks. I've only been late once. I'm sleeping better and my brain's gone much more quiet. I've caught up with most of the work. This week I haven't used my little red card once, though I'm still hanging on to it.

One by one, I am stepping up the rungs of my own personal Ladder of Fear. And soon I'm going to reach the very top.

Then I'll step off.

I closed the book and twisted Mum's driving mirror round so I could see the face I suddenly felt like pulling. This last story made me think. In one way, it was cheering. It certainly made my needing one single day off school look like a doddle.

But in another way, it worried me. I thought about the people in my school, even my friends, and how much I don't know about their real feelings. No one is totally honest. I wasn't going to go back and tell everyone, 'I just didn't feel like coming. I woke up in the morning, and all I wanted was to stay home.'

Not that I'd got to do that. I'd been in the car all morning. Mum had more visits on her list and I had finished the only book I'd brought along.

I checked the time on the dashboard. Ten minutes, Mum had said. This visit had already lasted longer than that.

I kept the mirror turned so I could watch the path, and finally I saw her hurrying back.

She threw herself in the car. 'Thank God that's over! Miserable, ungrateful, nit-picking trout!' She took a moment to collect herself then turned to give me a stern look. 'You never heard me say that!'

'No. Most unprofessional.' I grinned. I've heard Mum making work calls often enough to know the language she's supposed to use. 'It's not at all the sort of thing someone like you would ever say about a valued client.'

She smiled at me. 'Hungry again? Shall we pick up a sandwich?'

We drove back round the park and then along the busy road beside the shops. People in suits were rushing into coffee and sandwich shops. I checked the time again. Almost one o'clock.

'I could go in for second lunch sitting.'

'At school? What time is that?'

'Ten past.'

'Are you sure?'

'Which? Sure that the second sitting is at ten past, or sure I want to go?'

'Sure that you want to go. Because you're very welcome to stay with me. You've been no trouble. I've enjoyed your company.'

'I'll have days off more often,' I offered generously. 'Especially if we can stay home. But right now I've run out of book. And I am bored.'

'I can't stop near the roundabout,' she warned. 'But I could drop you off behind the brewery. You'd have to put on quite a turn of speed across the park to get there in time.'

'I can do that.' I grinned. 'It's not as if I'm one of your crumbling clients.'

'Right you are.'

As we crawled past the roadworks on the round-about approach, she nodded at *Away From Home*. 'So was it good?'

'I learned a lot,' I said, adding, to tease her, 'Far more than in three hours of school.'

She wasn't buying that. 'Come off it, Sam. Cake walks! Metaphorical. The number of roundabouts in Milton Keynes! *Folie à deux!*'

I let her think that what I'd said was just a joke. I couldn't think of any way I could explain. After all, none of the stories in the book had anything at all to do with me. Still, I had meant it when I said to her I'd learned a lot. Because I had. Not just about the people in the book who were away from home. About a load of other things. Mum's job. Old people's problems. Why the Satnav wasn't fixed. Mum's worries about Dad, and how she deals with them.

Even about myself.

Maybe next blue moon day I'd talk to her about all that.

⋆ ⋆ ⋆

So that is where she left me, at the brewery. It was a terrific run across the park. Nice cool crisp air. I felt myself bursting with what I thought was end-of-being-cooped-up energy, and then I realized it was confidence. I wasn't worried any more about Dad coming home. I'd realized Mum had things in hand. She knows him well enough to offer him a bit of leeway while he's settling in with both of us again – a bit like an astronaut having to adjust after re-entry.

But then, as always, she'll be firm enough to tell him what she expects (just as she does with me). And Dad will fall in line the way he always does, because he loves her just as much as she loves him.

We'll be the same well-oiled, grit-free family machine we were before.

I reached the back school gate. I got a couple of sharp words about not being in proper uniform. But that was all. (An easier re-entry than Dad has ever had!)

'You're lucky,' Mandy said as we were standing side by side at the tail end of the lunch queue. 'Mrs Crawford's off sick, so bits of the timetable have been switched round. You've just missed double maths. And we are doing art all afternoon.'

I'm brilliant at maths. And I hate art. So that'll teach me to bunk off.

Still, I enjoyed the book.

About the author

Anne Fine is one of our most distinguished writers for children. She has written over fifty highly acclaimed books and has won numerous awards, including the Guardian Children's Fiction Prize and both the Whitbread Children's Book of the Year and the Carnegie Medal twice over. Anne was appointed the Children's Laureate from 2001–3, and her work has been translated into over forty languages. In 2003 she became a Fellow of the Royal Society of Literature and was awarded an OBE. Anne lives in County Durham.

Have you read these other

books by Anne Fine?

BLOOD FAMILY

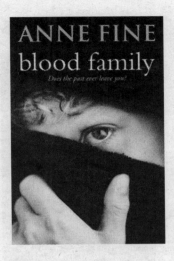

SHORTLISTED FOR THE CARNEGIE MEDAL

Edward is four years old when he is locked away by
his mother's violent boyfriend. By the time a neighbour
spots his pale face peering through a crack in the
boarded-up window, he is seven.

Rescue comes, but lasting damage has been done.
Years on, it's clear to Edward's new adoptive family
that something in his past haunts him still.

Then Edward catches sight of a photograph t
shocks him to the core.

Could there be another monster in his lif
been waiting to break out all al

'Superb' *Guardian*

THE DEVIL WALKS

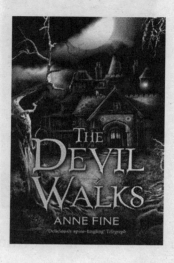

Since the day he was born, Daniel has been hidden
away from the outside world. Told that he suffers
from a mysterious illness, only a forceful knock at
the door reveals just how many secrets his silent
and reclusive mother has kept from him – and
how many lies she has told. Yet Daniel cannot
understand what she has tried to protect him
from so desperately.

Torn from the only home he has ever known,
Daniel begins to piece together the chilling truth
– a dark legacy of vicious cruelty and fiendish spite
that has held his family in its grip for years.

'A pitch-perfect Gothic thriller' *Sunday Telegraph*

UP ON CLOUD NINE

How stupid do you have to be to fall out of a top-floor window? Or was Stolly trying something else – up on cloud nine, even then?

Stolly has always been so alive: taking risks, hiding nothing, notorious for his imagination – and for his lies. But now he's lying in a hospital bed and Ian, his best friend, is watching, waiting and remembering . . .

'Anne Fine on top form' *Observer*

CHARM SCHOOL

It's the very last thing Bonny wants to do – but she has no choice.

Forced to spend a day at Charm School, Bonny is thrown head-first into a strange world of glitter and sparkle, silk and pearls – and the most self-obsessed little princesses she's ever met. Bonny tries to make friends, but every other girl is desperate to win Miss Opalene's Glistering Tiara – and they'll do anything to get it.

'Assured and lively' *Sunday Times*

THE ROAD OF BONES

SHORTLISTED FOR THE CARNEGIE MEDAL

In Yuri's country, people vanish. And no one ever comes back.

Now Yuri too is on a road to despair. A road built on the bones of those who dared to oppose ...

A chilling adventure from a multi–award–winning author.

'Evocative and convincing' *Sunday Times*